"Are you volunteering for the job?"

She rolled her eyes. "Of course not. I barely know you." She averted her gaze, willing away the memory of what took place in the kitchen just minutes ago. His touch affected her, and she hated to admit it.

He chuckled. "Seriously, God knows the future, and I trust Him to bring the right woman into our lives when He sees fit."

"Until then?"

"Until then, I'm a single dad."

"Well, that's where we differ. You see, my belief is that fathers can't nurture children the way mothers do. Women can single-handedly raise kids to become well-adjusted, productive citizens while men fall short of the mark time and time again."

ANDREA BOESHAAR and her husband Daniel have three adult sons, two of whom are married. Andrea attended college, first at the University of Wisconsin–Milwaukee, where she studied English, and then at Alverno College where she studied Professional Communications and Business Management.

Andrea has been writing stories and poems since she was a little girl; however, it wasn't until 1991, after she became a Christian, that she answered God's call to write exclusively for the Christian market. Since then Andrea has written articles, devotionals, novels, and novellas—many of which have made the CBA Bestseller List. For more on Andrea and a list of her published works, visit her web site at www.andreaboeshaar.com.

HEARTSONG PRESENTS

Books under the pen name Andrea Shaar
HP079—An Unwilling Warrior

Books by Andrea Boeshaar
HP188—An Uncertain Heart
HP238—Annie's Song
HP270—Promise Me Forever
HP279—An Unexpected Love
HP301—Second Time Around
HP342—The Haven of Rest
HP359—An Undaunted Faith
HP381—Southern Sympathies
HP401—Castle in the Clouds

HP428—An Unmasked Heart
HP466—Risa's Rainbow
HP541—The Summer Girl
HP582—The Long Ride Home
HP686—Always A Bridesmaid
HP742—Prescription for Love
HP798—Courting Disaster

Don't miss out on any of our super romances. Write to us at the following address for information on our newest releases and club information.

Heartsong Presents Readers' Service
PO Box 721
Uhrichsville, OH 44683

Or visit www.heartsongpresents.com

The Superheroes Next Door

Andrea Boeshaar

Heartsong Presents

For Daniel, Benjamin, Richard, and Brian...
You're all superheroes in my eyes!

A note from the Author:
I love to hear from my readers! You may correspond with me by writing:

Andrea Boeshaar
Author Relations
PO Box 721
Uhrichsville, OH 44683

ISBN 978-1-60260-191-8

THE SUPERHEROES NEXT DOOR

Our mission is to publish and distribute inspirational products offering exceptional value and biblical encouragement to the masses.

PRINTED IN THE U.S.A.

one

Perfect.

Ciara Rome scrutinized the row of two-story, red brick townhouses that spanned an entire block and concluded she'd made the right decision in renting the fourth home from the corner for the summer. A quiet neighborhood in a gated condo community was exactly what she wanted.

Several birds twittered in a nearby treetop, and a breeze caressed her face and neck. Only the gentle rustling of leafy branches could be heard.

Just perfect!

Gathering her belongings from her compact car, Cici's mind fast-forwarded to August when she anticipated handing in her master's thesis, all spit and polished, to an extremely pleased professor. How proud Professor Agnes Carter-Hill would be of her work. It had taken Cici years to nurture her theme and collect the evidence to support it. In all diligence, she'd persevered, completing the master's program at a university here in Iowa. She'd honed her supposition and then, with Aggie's guidance, she'd refined it. *The inconsequential effects of paternal absence on infants, preschool children, and teenagers.*

Essentially her hypothesis surmised that the male gender was unessential to quality childrearing, and it, of course, reflected Cici's personal belief as her mother had raised her single-handedly. Her father had left them when Cici was twelve. He moved away, never to be seen or heard from again. But who needed him, anyway? She and Mom had done all right for themselves. Mom had a decent-paying job as a supervisor for a housekeeping company in Nevada, and Cici was on the verge of attaining her master's degree.

She just needed to force herself to sit at the keyboard and

write up her thesis. And this peaceful subdivision would provide the perfect sabbatical in which to write it.

With the thick strap of her pink and black leather laptop case slung over her shoulder, Cici traipsed to the front door of the condo. She pulled her wheeled luggage behind her, then stopped and fished the key out of her jeans pocket. She could hardly wait to settle in and get started. She felt suddenly glad that her friend Jennifer Hargrove decided to rent out her condo while she celebrated her graduation with a trip across Europe with her fiancé and a few other couples they knew from their church. Cici had felt jealous that Jen earned her degree first, but the short-lived negative response soon gave way to genuine happiness and, once her own thesis was completed, Cici would celebrate her graduation. Then with any luck, she'd acquire a great-paying position within the Iowa Department of Education. She loved children and cared deeply about their welfare. She didn't need to trudge through foreign countries; a job with the Iowa DOE would be reward enough for her.

"Um, excuse me. . ."

Cici stood poised with the key in the door and was about to turn the lock when she heard a woman's voice coming up behind her.

She turned with a start and watched as a middle-aged woman with a stocky frame ambled up Jen's walkway.

"Pardon me. I didn't mean to give you a fright."

"Oh, um, no problem." Cici ran a hand over the top of her head, wondering if the woman had put a few gray hairs in its natural auburn color.

"I'm Roberta Rawlings. Welcome to Blossomwood Estates." She smiled and lifted her chin. Her gold and black animal print outfit seemed to accentuate her coppery eyes. "I'm the community director."

"Nice to meet you." Cici smiled politely. "I'm Ciara Rome. Cici for short. I'm renting Jennifer Hargrove's townhouse for the summer."

"Yes, I know." The older woman carefully tucked a lock of her chin-length brown hair behind her ear. "It's my job to know the comings and goings around here. It's what makes our community a safe one." Her smile grew. "And a fun one. I organize all the events, too."

Cici arched her brows. "Events?" Jen never said anything about organized events.

"Yes. We call it our Condo Club, and we have various social functions within our little community at least once a week. Practically everyone attends the functions."

"I see." Cici noticed the gleam of expectancy in Roberta's brown eyes and tried not to shudder. The last thing Cici wanted—or needed—was a social function forced upon her. Not when she had a thesis to write by August.

"I hope you won't be a stranger."

"I guess I can try to show up." Cici didn't want to seem unsociable and inadvertently tarnish Jen's good name with her neighbors.

"The Condo Club's next get-together is Friday evening."

Cici had a hunch the woman wouldn't take "no" for an answer.

"We'll have food and some fun games for the kids," she persisted. "I imagine you're eager to meet your neighbors. I mean, a woman should always know who's living next door." Roberta stepped closer. "For security purposes, of course."

"Oh, right."

"A woman can't be too careful these days."

"I suppose that's true enough."

Roberta replied with a curt nod as if to say, "Of course it is." Next, she shifted her stance. "Well, here's your welcome packet. The dates for all the events are listed in the folder."

"Thanks."

Cici watched Roberta turn and sashay down the walk, her skinny high-heeled shoes smacking on the cement with each step. With a sigh, Cici returned her attention to the front door and unlocked it. Cool, still air met her as she entered the condo.

Alone at last!

She took in the familiar surroundings and missed her friend all over again. She and Jen met in college at Iowa State University, located north of the city of Des Moines. They were best friends and did everything together, from adjusting to dorm life to making a home out of their first apartment. They'd studied, occasionally double-dated, and even spent holidays with each other's families. Cici's family consisted of only herself and Mom, but Jen made up for it because she was like the sister Cici never had.

Closing the door behind her, she walked through the adequately sized living room and made her way up the carpeted steps. Seeing the framed collage of Jen's family members and friends, Cici remembered back to that happy day when she and Jen had earned their bachelor's degrees. Later, they each decided to go on for their master's. However, something weird happened to Jen about two years ago: She found religion. Things just hadn't been quite the same since. Suddenly Jen no longer enjoyed frequenting their favorite nightclubs. Instead she found pleasure in going to church, of all things! Cici had visited a few "worship services" with her friend and found it inspiring in many ways, although it certainly wasn't her idea of a good time. She mentioned the experience to Aggie, who took an intellectual approach to Jen's finding faith in God. "Religion is a crutch upon which weak and narrow-minded people need to lean."

Cici wondered over her professor's remark ever since. Jen never seemed "weak and narrow-minded" before. But was she really? Had friendship blinded Cici to the fact?

Still deep in thought, she ambled into the master bedroom where she deposited her luggage. The yellow room felt bright and sunny. The beautiful multicolored quilt Jen had purchased at a local craft fair covered the queen-size bed. Cici took note of the large framed artwork hanging above it. Where had Jen found the atrocious thing? The print depicted a host of angels, warring in the heavens, while below an entire town went about its business, oblivious to the battle going on beyond the clouds.

Dramatic. Wonder what Aggie would have to say about it. Cici felt her lips curve upward in a smirk. Her distinguished professor would, no doubt, liken the artwork to some sort of cartoon.

But would she be right?

Cici shook off her musing and gazed around the bedroom. She paused at Jen's mirrored dresser. Several framed photographs adorned its polished oak surface. Making her way over, Cici lifted the picture of Jen standing beside her fiancé, William. Not Bill. Not Will. *William.* He was a husky, blond, Bible-quoting and -toting guy, and Jen was head over heels in love with him.

With a long sigh, Cici set the photo back in its place. As dogmatic as William could be about his faith, he seemed like a decent human being. What's more, her best friend loved him, so that was all the reason Cici needed to like the man. In fact, she looked forward to standing up in their wedding in October.

My thesis will be done long before then. I'll have completed another goal in life. . . .

Leaving the bedroom, she walked across the hallway and entered the second bedroom, which served as both a guest room and Jen's office. An oak-framed daybed was pushed against the length of one wall, and the rest of the space was occupied by a desk, bookcase, file cabinet, and built-in shelves on the wall. It looked completely functional. But best of all, it would be quiet, unlike the apartment Cici shared with two other friends. Jen had been the fourth roommate until she purchased this condo over a year ago. Cici often teased her, saying that she'd never forgive her for moving out and leaving Cici to fend for herself against Bridget and Tanya, two fun-loving females who enjoyed attending parties and nightclubs more than their classes at the university. However, they were honest, caring, loyal friends, and they paid their share of the rent on time. Even so, Cici understood Jen's need for her own place—a place she could call home. She'd found it here in this condo. . . .

And someday, Cici vowed, she'd have that, too. A home of her own—

Just as soon as she wrote her thesis.

❧

Luke Weldon sat on the edge of the bathtub, helping his three young sons dry off and get into their pajamas. Exhaustion weighted his every limb, every muscle. He felt as though he'd melt down the side of the tub and land in a pool of fatigue all over the ceramic tile floor. He'd worked all day, trying to keep clients happy with their software products, but he still had more to do. His sister-in-law had only been able to watch the boys for a few hours this afternoon, and while he was grateful for the help, it hadn't been long enough. Now he'd be forced to work all night—once he got the kids to sleep, that is.

Another all-nighter. That was the trouble with a home-based business. A guy couldn't pack up and leave the office at the end of the day. Instead, his business followed him day and night.

He glanced at the happy, earnest expressions on his kids' faces as they raced to be the first one in their pj's. Devin, of course, would win—as he usually did. At the mature and responsible age of six and a half, he was eighteen months older than his twin brothers, Aaron and Brian. He was his daddy's helper—but they all were. They'd had to be—ever since that tragic night when Alissa was killed.

He squeezed his eyes closed. *Why, God? Why did that accident have to happen? Most of all, why couldn't I have been enough for her—me and our babies?*

Luke stymied his thoughts. He'd asked those questions a million times since Alissa's death, and he knew from experience that such inquiries only brought on a selfish pity party. Luke had no time for those. Not anymore.

Father, forgive me for questioning Your sovereignty. Silently Luke added Job's words. *"I know that You can do everything, and that no purpose of Yours can be withheld from You."*

"I win!"

Luke snapped his attention to dark-haired Devin, who stood with his arms up in victory. He was in his Spiderman pj's while Brian and Aaron tied for second place, one wearing Batman pajamas and the other, Superman.

"Come on, heroes," Devin declared, bolting out of the bathroom. "We've got work to do."

The younger boys followed, arms stretched out, pretending they were flying.

Luke grinned and sopped up the water that had spilled over from the "rub-a-dub-dub, three men in a tub" bath time and hung the wet towels over the ceramic wall racks to dry. He gathered up the plastic toys and put them in a netted bag hooked over the faucet.

Then he sucked in a breath and blew it out again. His sons were whooping it up, and he knew what they were up to.

"Better not be jumping on my bed." Luke had to grin in spite of himself.

Laughter turned to whispers and giggles.

Praying for a second wind, Luke made his way down the hallway and into his room where precious faces peered up at him. He recognized the mischief shining in all three pairs of deep brown eyes.

"You were jumping on my bed, weren't you?" Luke placed his hands on his hips, trying to act stern.

The boys just looked at him.

"Won't fess up, huh? Fine. Now you're all going to get it."

He inched forward and feigned a menacing expression. All three boys grinned in anticipation. They knew what was coming. When Luke reached the bed, he shot out his hands and tickled them all at the same time while flinging his own body over the width of the king-sized bed. The boys jumped all over him like puppies, squealing in delight.

Ignoring the protests from his weary body, Luke laughed and played with abandon.

two

All she wanted was some peace and quiet! Was that really too much to ask?

First Roberta Rawlings' phone message this morning, reminding her about the get-together on Friday and then these kids next door.

Cici lazed back in the tan leather chair and tossed her silver-plated, monogrammed pen onto the desk. Frustration caused her temples to throb. She'd put up with the noise next door all day; she was tempted to contact Roberta Rawlings—or even e-mail Jen—and complain. Cici had wanted a sabbatical and now here she sat, making corrections on her printed copy before she typed them into her laptop computer. The only problem was the rambunctious children next door. Jen had also failed to mention her noisy neighbors.

The boisterous laughter reverberated from behind the shared wall of the connected homes. She imagined at least a dozen of them over there, jumping on the beds and throwing pillows and toys. It sounded as though they'd soon come bursting through the plaster and land in her office.

A thunderous *boom* sounded, rattling the picture on the wall above the desk. Then Cici heard a horrendous *crash*. Sudden silence followed, and she figured the kids must have broken something. Where in the world was their mother?

Things on the other side of the wall remained quiet, and the opportunity to get back to work presented itself, but Cici's concentration had been hopelessly broken. She stared, unseeing, at the computer screen in front of her and forced herself to imagine how terrific she'd feel when she handed in her completed thesis. She envisioned reaching her goal.

I can do this. Cici tried to psych herself up and dive into her work again. However, she couldn't keep from wondering if the children next door were all right. What if they'd been left alone? She'd heard countless reports about parents leaving their kids unattended. What if the youngsters burned the place down?

Fear gripped her. What if that really happened and her computer was damaged in the fire? What if she lost her thesis and all her research?

A sense of urgency shot through her, and Cici stood. As she made her way downstairs, she became engaged in self-debate. Was this really a good idea? She didn't want to be a busybody neighbor. Then again, she didn't want the children's welfare endangered, not to mention anyone else's if something disastrous did occur.

It's about being responsible, she finally reasoned.

Her mind made up, she opened the back door and stepped out onto the cement-slab patio. Cici inhaled the fresh air and noticed the sky was a perfect blue. The sunshine spilled into the spacious yard and glittered off something on the wooden play structure with its swings, bright yellow slide, and colorful awning. The kid in Cici begged for release, but she squelched it like she'd done ever since she was twelve. After her dad left, Cici grew up fast. She'd had to.

Painful memories threatened, but she quickly shook them off and focused on her thesis—and the very reason she was trekking over to her next-door neighbor's house.

She walked around the cedar partition that separated the two patios and provided a bit of privacy from the adjoining two-story condo. She reached the neighbor's white-paneled back door and rang the bell. A full minute ticked by during which she swatted at several pesky flies. Pressing the doorbell again, she continued to wait until, finally, a dark-haired child with large, curious brown eyes opened the door and peered through the crack.

"Hi." Cici cleared her throat. "I'm living next door, and—"

The door opened wider and a taller but similar-looking

child stared back at her. Cici spotted their blue jeans, shirtless chests, and then noticed the blankets tied around their necks. She hid a grin.

Suddenly another little fellow appeared, shouting, "We're defenders of the universe!"

He ran back inside, disappearing as fast as he'd shown up.

Cici's amusement fled as she glanced at the two remaining caped crusaders. She imagined the lack of control in the house. "Who's watching over you kids?"

"Jesus!" the smaller boy shouted out as if he were answering a Sunday school quiz question.

Cici refrained from rolling her eyes. Things here might be worse than she imagined. "Is there a *real* adult in the house?" If not, she planned to call Social Services.

"Can I help you?"

A man, tall with a medium build and the most incredible mahogany-brown eyes Cici had ever seen, suddenly stood at the door. His dark hair fell over his forehead and ears, spilling onto his neck in a stylishly mussed but masculine fashion.

The two boys scampered away and the man, who appeared every inch a "real adult," stepped forward. He wore a light blue button-down shirt that hung over faded jeans.

"I'm Luke Weldon. What can I do for you?"

"Well, um, I just moved in next door. I'm—"

"Ciara." A broad smile split Luke's suntanned face. "Jen told me you were coming for the summer." He unlocked the screen door and swung it open. "Come on in."

Stunned, Cici fought the invitation. She'd come over here to complain about the noise, after all. "I'm working on my master's thesis, and—"

"Yeah, yeah, come on in before the flies do." Lightly touching Cici's elbow, he steered her toward the kitchen. "My kids have been eating their frozen juice treats outside, and I haven't had a chance to hose off the patio, so the flies are fierce."

"So I noticed." Cici forced a polite smile. She took in her surroundings, noticing the dishes piled in the sink and the partially eaten peanut butter and jelly sandwiches left on paper plates on the round kitchen table. "How many kids live here?"

"Three."

Only three?

Luke seemed to follow her gaze. "Pardon the mess. I've been repairing a software program all morning. It's not doing what I designed it to and, needless to say, the company that purchased it hasn't been pleased. But I think I've got it up and running now. I could use a little break." He made his way to the refrigerator. "Want a soda?"

"No, thanks. The truth is I've been working on my master's thesis all morning and—"

"So you could use a break, too, huh?" He flipped open a soda can and took a swig. "I'm glad you came over to get acquainted."

"Well, to tell you the truth, I—"

The volume on the television suddenly soared to a deafening blare. Cici jumped. One of the kids ran into the kitchen, his little face masked with concern as if a true crisis were at hand.

"Dad, Aaron's playing with the remote again!" He ran back into the living room.

"'Scuse me." Luke set down his soda and followed the boy out of the kitchen.

Scenes from the flick, *Mr. Mom,* flitted through Cici's head as the volume on the TV went down. She laughed to herself, recalling the countless times she'd watched that movie. One of her roommates owned the DVD. But, however funny the story line, the premise reinforced Cici's theory that a guy just couldn't run a house single-handedly, raise well-adjusted children, and maintain a career.

But a woman could. In fact, women didn't need men at all when it came to raising children, and kids survived just fine without a father.

She had.

Minutes passed, and finally Luke strolled back into the

kitchen. "Sorry about that. I had to deal with my son."

Cici arched a brow. "Deal with him?"

Luke smiled. "Discipline him. He's not allowed to play with the television or the remote and he disobeyed."

"Hmm. . ." Cici found it interesting that she hadn't heard any sort of scolding. "Well, I'll bet you'll be glad when your wife gets home."

Luke took another swig of his canned soft drink. "I'm not married."

"Oh, so you're divorced? Your day to have the kids?"

He shook his head. "My wife died a few years ago."

His reply stunned her. "I–I'm sorry. . ."

"Thanks." A mix of discomfort and gloom settled over his features.

"I'm sure you miss her very much."

"Yeah." He sucked in a breath and blew it out again. "But I can't change the past. What's more, I have three sons to raise and a business to run, so I can't very well sit around feeling sorry for myself."

"No, I suppose you can't." She regarded him askance. "Are you raising your boys on your own?"

"Yes, but I have help from my in-laws and friends at church."

Cici had to admit she admired his candor. However, his mention of "friends at church" gave her an uneasy feeling.

"In fact, Jen and William babysat for me so I could attend a seminar."

"They did, huh?" Her suspicion mounted. "So, you've met William?"

"He's one of my best friends."

Cici hid a grimace. Her inkling had been correct. Another religious kook. She should have figured—except Jen never mentioned the single father next door. Unless. . .

She tamped down the sudden swell of enthusiasm. Luke Weldon might be living proof that her master's theory was correct. It was sheer brilliance on Jen's part. Obviously it had been her plan all along. Except. . .it didn't quite make sense given that Jen heartily disagreed with Cici's viewpoint.

Unless Jen had another plan in mind.

Cici squared her shoulders. "Just so you know, William has already preached to me, so you can save your breath."

A frown furrowed his dark brows. "What are you talking about?"

"You know very well what I'm talking about. If you know William and you've got church friends, then you're one of them. You're a Christian. And Christians feel some kind of need to convert the world to their narrow-minded way of thinking. But I have my own way, my own religion."

"All right." He lifted a shoulder. "I can respect that."

Cici brought herself up, fully expecting more of an argument out of him. When none came, she relaxed and reminded herself why she came over here in the first place.

"Um, getting back to the reason I came over. . ." She placed her hands on her hips. "As I said, I'm writing my master's thesis." Cici noticed the kids were trickling into the room, one by one, and watching her with their gorgeous, wide brown eyes. She saw the intelligence in their depths, and she saw something else, too. Something she couldn't quite explain. "So, like I said, I was working on my thesis, and I had to stop because of. . ."

She paused again, unable to complain about the noise while the boys stood by staring at her. She decided she could never hurt their feelings. "Well, I heard kids playing, and I wanted to come over and say hello. I like kids." She brought her gaze back to Luke. "I hope to get a job with the Iowa Department of Education once I've completed school. I just have my thesis left to write and then I'm finished."

"Good for you." His gaze traveled over the tops of his children's heads. "Let me introduce my boys. This is Devin." He placed his hand on the tallest boy's shoulder. "He's six."

"Almost seven," Devin corrected. "My birthday is October seventeenth, and I'll be in first grade this year."

"I'm impressed." Cici smiled at the boy.

"I'm Aaron." One of the twins stepped forward, and with the light blue blanket still caped around his neck, he raised both arms as if showing off his muscles. "I'm a superhero!"

And the one who likes to play with the TV's remote control. Cici grinned.

"I'm a superhero, too," the other twin added before shyly ducking behind Luke.

"Tell Miss Ciara your name," he prompted. "She's going to live in Miss Jenny's house for the summer."

"Brian," the boy blurted before hiding his face again.

"The twins are five years old."

"I'm a superhero, too," Devin informed her. "But I do more superheroing around here cuz I'm the oldest."

"I'm a superhero, too," Luke mimicked, earning perplexed stares from his children.

Finally the little firecracker spoke up. "Da—ad," Aaron said, "you can't b'tend you're a superhero, cuz you're big." He gave Luke's hip a playful shove.

Not to be outdone, the other boys copied their brother.

"Hey, don't beat me up. I'm not a bad guy." He tickled the kids and they dissolved into fits of giggles.

Cici couldn't help smiling as she looked on.

"Okay, that's enough goofing around. We have a guest, remember? That means we're on our best behavior."

The boys righted themselves and looked back at Cici.

"Listen, it's nice to meet you superheroes. All of you." She locked her gaze with Luke's. She had to admit he was an exceptionally fine-looking man, and she admired his good-humored manner. Clearly, his kids adored him. However, those traits alone didn't qualify him to be a sole parent. Children needed a mother's nurturing and real discipline, coaching, and encouragement in order to become productive citizens and lead successful lives. They didn't need to grow up parented by Peter Pan, and she hoped to prove it in her thesis.

"So tell me." She copped a sassy attitude and folded her arms. "How do you know I'm a 'Miss'?"

"What?" Luke appeared confused.

"You've introduced me as *Miss Ciara*."

"Oh, that's easy." His lips curved upward mischievously, and he gave her a charming wink. "Us superheroes know everything."

three

Hands on hips, Luke stood at the large picture window in his living room and peered out at his new neighbor. She was speaking with Tori Evenrod from the condo across the street, and Luke couldn't drag his gaze away from her.

Ciara. She had the most beautiful name he'd ever heard and it fit her. She was altogether unforgettable.

Luke expelled a disappointed sigh as he watched the slender redhead conversing on the walk. That gorgeous, thick, wavy hair of hers was piled on her head, secured with some sort of clip, and she wore faded blue jeans and a sleeveless white shirt.

Don't look too close. She's not a believer, Luke reminded himself. Neither William nor Jen had mentioned whether Ciara was a Christian or not, but she had made it clear enough to him yesterday. She said she had her "own religion."

I've got no business entertaining my attraction to this woman.

In spite of his self-reproof, he couldn't help staring. She stood close enough so he could see her blue eyes widen at something Tori said, and he recalled the freckles sprinkled across Ciara's pretty face and slim arms. She had the kind of skin that seemed like it would sunburn easily.

Luke shook himself and captured his wayward thoughts before turning from the window. "What am I thinking?" He smacked his palm to his forehead. He had work to do, and here he stood, wasting time, gawking at his neighbor. In only a few hours, the kids would return home from the public pool. They'd gone swimming with friends this afternoon.

Taking the steps two at a time, Luke made his way up to his office. He decided it might be a good idea for him to stay away from Ciara Rome—as far away as possible.

❧

Cici dragged herself to the Condo Club's Friday evening get-together. She'd needed the break from working at her computer all day, and she figured it wouldn't hurt to meet a few more of Jen's neighbors. So far she liked Tori Evenrod. She found the woman amusing, and Tori had the scoop on everyone in her little community.

Cici was particularly interested in getting the lowdown on Luke Weldon. After meeting him, she'd decided to act on her idea that he and his adorable but incredibly rambunctious kids would make perfect examples, serving as further proof her thesis was correct. Now she planned to set about obtaining her data. Of course that meant hanging around with a religious nut for a while, but Cici figured she could handle it, seeing as how she loved Jen as a sister and she could tolerate William. What's more, according to Tori, Luke was a "good guy" and a target for several of the single women in the neighborhood. Cici understood she had stiff competition in vying for Luke's time.

She smiled. Nothing like a good challenge.

"Hey, I haven't seen you around before."

Cici turned to see a blond, burly guy standing to her right. He wore tight-fitting jeans and a white T-shirt that bore the name of a popular beer across the chest.

"You must not come to these things often." He gave her a lazy grin. "Either that or you just moved in."

"Both, actually." Cici pushed out a polite smile. "I'm renting a friend's condo for the summer."

"Oh." A curious light sparked in his blue eyes, and a smile split his weather-worn, tanned face. Then he stuck out his right hand. "The name's Chase Tibbits."

"Ciara Rome." She slipped her palm into his and noticed his hand's calloused texture. She imagined he was some sort of contractor. "Nice to meet you."

"Hey, same here."

"What do you do for a living, Mr. Tibbits?"

He guffawed and several heads turned. "I'm no 'mister.' Call me Chase." He chuckled once more. "I do roofing, siding. You name it, I can do it."

"Can you knit? Crochet?" Cici couldn't seem to stifle the quip.

"Everything except those things." Chase laughed. "Needles scare me. Nails don't—unless they're fingernails."

"Funny." Cici grinned.

He grunted out a laugh before glancing over at the food table in a shady part of the condo clubhouse's yard. "Hey, would you like a beer?"

She tipped her head, noting that he enjoyed using the word *hey*. "No, thanks." She wanted to get back to her thesis, and she knew an alcoholic beverage would only cloud her thinking.

"Well, I'm going to get another one. I'll be back."

"Take your time."

Chase strode off to get a drink and, moments later, Cici spied Luke and his boys. The kids appeared well-groomed, each attired in a brightly colored shorts outfit. She couldn't help noticing that Luke, also, looked nice in his khaki slacks and tan polo shirt. His dark hair had been neatly combed, although a few rakish strands hung over his forehead.

Smiling, she made her way toward him. "Well, hi, neighbor."

"Hi, Ciara." Luke gave her a warm smile. He prompted his boys to tell her hello, which they immediately did.

"Daddy, we're hungry," Devin complained.

Before Luke could reply, a beautiful woman with Mediterranean features cut in. "I'll get the kids some food." Her almond-shaped brown eyes darkened with an unspoken but suggestive invitation. "You know how much I adore your kids. . . ."

Cici guessed the woman was ready and willing to move into the wife and mommy role at the Weldon house.

"And Roberta outdid herself with the snack table tonight. There's all sorts of food that your boys will love."

"No, thanks, Michayla, but I appreciate the offer." He took hold of his two youngest sons' hands. Then he introduced Cici.

"If you'll excuse me now, I need to feed my children."

"Of course." Cici watched the Weldons walk away before returning her gaze to the black-haired woman.

"Nice to meet you."

"Likewise."

Michayla Martinelli relaxed her stance, although she maintained a certain measure of aloofness. "New in the neighborhood?"

"Yes. I'm renting a friend's condo for the summer." Cici wished she could have pasted a sign across her forehead so she wouldn't have to repeat the same information over and over.

"Only for the summer?"

"Right."

"What a shame." Michayla's tone rang with gentle sarcasm. Then she feigned a little smile. "Although, fall is my favorite time of year."

Cici ignored the subtle insult. She couldn't care less what the woman thought about her and whether she had targeted Luke Weldon as her next conquest. Cici had moved into Jen's condo for one thing and one thing only: to write her thesis.

Chase returned with a drink in his hand.

"Hey, Mic, how's it going?" He hugged her around the shoulders.

In reply, she gave him a withering glare before shrugging out of his hold and striding off.

Chase chuckled. "She idolizes me."

"I can see that," Cici quipped, although she couldn't help wondering if Chase was for real. Was his ego the size of Montana or had he purposely goaded the lovely Michayla Martinelli for sheer entertainment?

Cici rather suspected the answer to her question was both ego and entertainment. She also had to admit that Chase was attractive in a rather brutish sort of way.

"Hey, you never did tell me what you do."

"What I do? As in my career?"

"Yeah." The dimple in his right cheek winked at her as he smiled. "Let me guess: You're a teacher."

"No, but I've done some teaching, right before I managed a day care center. Now I'm finishing up my master's thesis."

She expounded on her topic but soon realized Chase's mind, as well as his gaze, had wandered. Cici didn't waste another word on him. Instead, she strolled over to Tori Evenrod, conversed for a bit, and met several more individuals.

Then, as fate would have it, she ran into Luke Weldon again.

"Having fun?"

"I don't know about 'fun,' but it's been a pleasant evening." She glanced at her wristwatch, contemplating leaving the party and heading for Jen's condo.

"Did you get something to eat?"

"Not much." Cici had indulged in a diet cola and a few crackers with cheese spread, and that had kept her hunger at bay. She figured she'd eat back at Jen's condo. "What about you?"

"The boys are eating. They loved those miniature meatballs." He grinned and glanced around at the mingling crowd. "I see you met both Michayla and Chase."

"Sure did."

"And you're not running for cover?" Luke stuck his hands into the pockets of his tan trousers. "I'm impressed. They're two of the neighborhood's more, um, volatile residents."

Cici couldn't help teasing him. She folded her arms and grinned. "Why would I be intimidated with *Superman* here?"

The retort earned her one of Luke's captivating smiles. "And, speaking of superheroes, I s'pose I should get mine home."

"I was just leaving myself. Can I walk with you?"

"Absolutely."

Luke swung around and Cici followed his gaze to where

his sons were sitting with other kids. Next, without warning, Luke blew out an ear-ringer of a whistle.

Cici cringed, but the Weldon boys came running. They stood before their dad like soldiers awaiting orders from their commander in chief.

"Time to go home."

They moaned, but the well-mannered superheroes didn't actually complain.

She fell in step beside Luke, feeling more convinced than ever that a woman was responsible for instilling such admirable character traits in the kids. Surely Luke just benefited from what she'd done—whoever "she" was.

"You mentioned getting a lot of help with your boys. Female help, huh?"

Luke seemed to mull over the question for several seconds. "Well, my sister-in-law watches the guys if she's got a day off, and, like today, Nancy Smith, a neighbor, took my kids to the public swimming pool along with her brood."

It wasn't quite the answer Cici was digging for and, as if sensing her dissatisfaction, Luke added, "I don't have a harem, if that's what you're asking, and I certainly would never use my kids in order to get a woman to date me."

Cici replied with an ambivalent shrug, telling herself she wasn't impressed either way. She'd known her share of lying, cheating men—men like her own father—and she wasn't convinced Luke couldn't be lumped into that category.

"And if it's Michayla's solicitousness that prompted your question," Luke continued, "I'm not interested in accepting her offers, kind as they may sound, because I know there are strings attached. Strings I have no intentions of getting tangled up in. I might be a simple Christian man, but I'm not stupid."

"Guess time will tell, won't it? I mean, I don't think any man can refuse a woman like Michayla forever." She nudged him with her elbow and grinned. "Not even a superhero like you."

"You're totally wrong." A smug smile curved his lips and he

shook his head. He kept his gaze up ahead at the kids who skipped, jumped, and ran in front of them. "And, if you must know, I don't find Michayla Martinelli particularly attractive."

Cici laughed in disbelief. "Okay, so maybe you're not stupid, but you must be blind."

"I'm neither, thank you very much." He slid a glance to her and then back at his sons.

A slight frown pulled at her brows. "Are you in a committed relationship with someone else?" she asked—as part of her research, of course.

"Nope. How about you?"

"Not at this time, no." The truth was, Cici hadn't ever been all that committed to any guy. Her education and furthering her career had taken precedence her entire adult life. Her roommates even went so far as to label her a "workaholic."

"So, um, what about Chase Tibbits?"

Cici peered over at Luke and glimpsed his mischievous grin.

"The women around here swoon over Chase just because he owns a lot of power tools, but I noticed you didn't seem too taken with him."

"I wasn't. He's not my type."

"Well, see, the same goes for me and Michayla. She's not my type." Luke halted in midstride, causing Cici to do the same.

"Did I get too personal? If so, I apologize." Cici meant it sincerely.

"No, it's not that." Luke shook his head, but Cici saw the curious gleam in his brown eyes. "I'm just wondering why in the world we're discussing Chase and Michayla, two of my least favorite neighbors."

"Oh, well I can explain my questions about Michayla." She cast a self-conscious smile at her sandals. "Let me explain. You see, I'm curious about the women who have impacted your sons' young lives. I'm still researching my master's thesis."

"Got it." Understanding lit Luke's eyes, and he began walking again. "Research. Okay, well, in that case. . ."

Once more Cici fell into step beside him.

"The boys' grandmas, Sunday school teachers, friends, and even neighbors—with the exception of two who, for research purposes, shall remain nameless. . ."

Cici couldn't help grinning.

"They've all impacted my kids in some way."

She and Luke reached their connecting units and strolled up the side walkway and around to the back. Cici decided that, in spite of herself, she found Luke quite engaging.

"Can I help you get the kids settled?"

"No, I can't ask you to do that." He paused at the end of the fence separating the two patios and handed the house key to Devin. "Especially not since I spent the last block convincing you that I don't use my kids as bait in order to capture a woman's interest." He tossed a glance skyward as if to emphasize the ridiculousness of the notion.

Cici laughed. "Well, then, it's a good thing you're not asking. I'm offering. Besides," she added, stepping around him, "I'm not interested in you. I like your kids."

"Oooh. . ."

Cici caught his playful wince.

"You sure know how to chink a superhero's armor."

four

"The place is a mess. I wasn't expecting company."

"I completely understand." Cici scanned the sink full of dirty dishes, the cluttered countertops, and the uncleared table. The apartment she shared with her roommates, Bridget and Tanya, could look this bad and, sometimes, worse. "Not to worry."

The boys ran into the living room and suddenly the television's volume boomed.

Cici jumped.

Devin bolted into the kitchen. "Dad!"

"I know, son. Aaron is playing with the remote again." Luke followed his son out of the kitchen.

In that moment, Cici experienced a sense of chaos like she'd never before imagined. But just as quickly, the TV's volume went down and Luke seemed to regain control of his household. The next thing Cici heard was the sound of three pairs of sneakers thundering up the carpeted steps. How could three little boys be so noisy?

Luke reentered the kitchen looking none the worse for wear. "I'm going to help the boys get into their pajamas. If you'd like to read them each a story before bedtime, that'd be appreciated."

"I'd love to." She cast a glance at the sink. "How 'bout if I start working on your dishes while you help the kids upstairs?"

"No way. You're my guest." He motioned to the living room. "Please. Have a seat, get comfy, and the kids will be down with their books in a few minutes. While you read to them, I can get the kitchen cleaned up."

"Okay, if you're sure. . ."

"I'm sure." Luke nodded toward the living room and gave her a quick grin before heading upstairs to tend to his boys.

Cici watched him go then strode out of the kitchen and sat down on the blue, white, and green plaid sofa. The upholstery had obviously seen better days and the pale blue carpet looked worn in places, too. But, overall, the living area seemed clean.

She listened to the commotion upstairs. The boys were fussing at each other. She heard Luke's mild-mannered tone reminding them there was a guest present and that they should be on their "best behavior."

She looked around, taking in her surroundings. Across the room, the television was encased in a cherry wood wall unit. An assortment of framed photographs and knickknacks occupied adjacent shelves. Just when she felt tempted to walk over and get a closer view, two of the three kids ran down the stairs, storybooks under their arms.

Devin, the oldest boy, sat to Cici's left and dropped his hard-covered book in her lap. "Can I go first?"

"Sure." She glanced at the book's title: *The Truck Book*. She looked at Devin. "You like trucks?"

He replied with a vigorous nod.

Brian, the shy twin, sat on Cici's right side. He slipped his book onto her legs and stared up at her with probing brown eyes. They held a depth that seemed beyond his years, and Cici felt a tug on her heartstrings.

She turned her attention to the title of his book. *"The Oak Inside the Acorn."* She gave the boy a smile. "Sounds interesting."

He replied with a nod and a shy smile.

"Where's your other brother?" she asked the two beside her.

"Aaron's getting a talking-to because he played with the remote again." Devin wore a serious expression. "But he and my dad will be down pretty soon."

"Okay, we'll wait."

A "talking-to," huh? Cici was curious and decided to quiz the children. "A 'talking-to' doesn't sound like much of a punishment. Do you ever get a time-out or lose privileges?"

"Sometimes." Again, Devin was the one to reply.

But before she could dig further, Aaron bounded down the steps, followed by his father.

"I'm going last." Aaron held up his book. Cici only glimpsed the title. Something about pirates who didn't do anything.

She frowned, wondering what the story could possibly be about.

"Dad said after the story we can watch the movie. That's why I don't care about going last."

"Movie? Yay!" Devin cheered and Brian was quick to join in.

Luke grinned and sat down in the dark blue upholstered armchair adjacent to where Cici sat on the sofa.

"Well, I guess I should get started so the kids can watch their movie." She looked his way for affirmation.

He gave her a nod.

"You don't have to read my book." Devin withdrew his choice from her lap. "I know how to read most of it myself anyhow, and I want to watch the movie."

"All right." She glanced at Luke to confirm the decision.

He shrugged in acquiescence.

Cici began reading Brian's selection. The story was all about how people have specific purposes in life and, therefore, they needed to be "the trees" that God made them to be.

Nothing wrong with the story's overall message, although Cici picked up on the religious propaganda sprinkled throughout its contents. She told herself she shouldn't be surprised.

"Well, wasn't that nice?" She closed the book.

"Yeah, and I think if I was a tree, I'd be like that oak tree," Devin remarked.

"Thank goodness you're a superhero instead," Cici teased with a look at Luke. He smiled back, and she had the feeling he wasn't at all interested in cleaning his kitchen. Instead he appeared thoroughly relaxed, enjoying story time as much as his kids.

"So, Devin"—she returned her attention to the soon-to-be first grader—"do you think God really cares what happens here on earth?" She wondered if Luke would object to her challenging his son's faith.

He didn't, and Devin was quick to answer.

"Yeah, He cares. He made us and I care about stuff I make, so why wouldn't God?"

Cici weighed the candid reply and found she couldn't argue with it. After all, she cared about things she created. . . like her thesis.

"What about you?" she asked Aaron, who sat at his father's feet. "Do you think God is really up in heaven somewhere, worrying about what's happening here on earth?"

"Yeah."

"How do you know?" She glanced at Luke again but didn't get the feeling that he minded her questions. She'd cease at once if she thought he objected.

"I don't know." Aaron raised his narrow shoulders. "I just know."

Because it's what you've been taught, and you haven't learned any differently.

"I know," Brian said.

Cici turned to regard him.

"He's real because God is love." Brian's brown eyes shone with earnestness. "My dad loves us like God does."

"Except God is perfect," Luke added, "and I'm just a regular guy."

"In heaven we'll be perfect kids," Devin said. "Aaron won't always get in trouble in heaven."

Aaron nodded as he peeked over his shoulder at his dad who sent him an affectionate wink.

Cici grew uncomfortable with the subject, although she couldn't say why. She'd discussed God, the Bible, and various Christian beliefs with Jen and William plenty of times in the past. Occasionally she and William would verbally spar over a particular point, mostly because Cici enjoyed razzing him. Jen always knew what she was up to, but William took the challenge each and every time. However, no matter the outcome, he never held a grudge. That spoke volumes about his character, in Cici's mind. But she scarcely knew Luke, and he didn't strike her as a guy who loved a good debate. He seemed more the peacekeeping kind, and she'd hate to offend him in his own home. "Okay, well, I think it's time to move on to the next book."

"I just wanna watch the movie." Aaron turned to look up at his dad again.

"Me, too," Devin said.

"Me, too!" Brian exclaimed.

The vote was unanimous, so Luke stood, strode across the room, and inserted the DVD into the player located beneath the TV. As he did so, he gave Cici a brief history of the VeggieTales animated characters. The kids expounded on his explanation with a high-spirited synopsis about the pirate movie. They had obviously seen it before.

"Basically it comes down to this. . ." Luke wrapped it up. "A hero doesn't have to be the bravest or the smartest. A hero just has to want to do what's right in God's eyes." He eyed his sons. "Right, guys?"

"Yeah, superheroes!" In all his excitement, Aaron stood and started running around the room until Luke cleared his throat.

"He's gonna get another talking-to," Brian whispered, wide-eyed, to Cici.

She said nothing. She just observed the boys and Luke and made mental notes as she watched them interact.

Finally Luke sat on the floor and pulled Aaron into his lap. He still wiggled and squirmed, although his dad's restraining arms kept the little bundle of energy contained so he couldn't disrupt his brothers during the movie.

Cici watched the DVD while surreptitiously observing Luke and the kids. The kids sang along with the vegetable-like characters dressed as pirates—and she concluded the flick smacked of more religious propaganda, albeit subtly. She couldn't deny, however, that it was cute, and the children appeared to thoroughly enjoy what they saw and heard.

When the movie ended, Luke directed the boys up to bed.

"Thanks for allowing me to barge in on you." Cici rose from the sofa. "I don't feel like I was much help to you."

"I've got a decent routine down when it comes to bedtime, but the boys are always excited to have someone besides me read them stories."

"Good. It was fun." Cici gave him a smile.

Luke returned the gesture as he stuffed his hands into the pockets of his khaki trousers. "Did you gain any new info for your research?"

"Yes, actually."

"Cool. I'm happy to answer any other questions you have on kids, not that I'm a huge expert or anything." He shifted from one foot to the other.

"Thanks." Cici pushed out a grin. Without the kids around as a buffer, things between her and Luke felt suddenly awkward.

"Well. . ." He bobbed his head and pursed his lips. "Um, I'd better get the kids into bed. But you're welcome to stay. Feel free to grab a cola or something out of the fridge."

Cici thought over the invitation. However, before she could reply, a thunderous crash sounded from above.

She glanced at the ceiling before sending Luke a wide-eyed stare.

He remained calm. "That would be Aaron, parachuting from his top bunk."

"Parachuting?"

Luke was halfway up the stairs already. "That's what he calls it. He throws his pillows and blankets onto the floor and then leaps off the top bunk. *Parachuting.*"

The idea made Cici gape while riotous laughter filled the second floor. No doubt the little daredevil and his brothers never thought of the dangers associated with such a stunt.

From where she stood, rooted to the carpet, she couldn't wait to see how Luke handled this situation. Would he yell? Spank? She knew what she'd do if she were in charge. She'd see to it the child lost some privileges beginning tomorrow morning!

She listened. Things upstairs didn't sound amiss. No angry voices. No crying. But the silence was deafening. Cici wondered what was happening and debated whether to leave or stay.

Within moments, the latter won out. She'd offered to help, after all. Besides, she was much too curious to go back to Jen's condo now.

Making her way into the kitchen, she opened the dishwasher and started loading it. She'd only rinsed a few sticky cups and set them in the top rack when Luke suddenly appeared.

"Hey, what are you doing?" He caught her wrists.

She looked up at him and their gazes locked. Cici felt pinned by his deep brown eyes. She saw them travel down her face and pause at her mouth, as her insides seemed to flip with anticipation while he gently held her wrists. Was he about to kiss her? In that split second, Cici didn't think she'd mind it at all. His nearness overwhelmed her senses in a dizzying way, and she felt certain he could hear her heart banging inside her rib cage. Whatever the intriguing, nameless, electrifying current was between them, it was mutual. Cici felt sure of at least that much.

But then Luke stepped back, dropped her hands, and the magic vanished.

Cici was both puzzled and disappointed.

"You're my guest." His tone sounded serious and his gaze backed it up. "I don't make my guests clean my kitchen."

"Make?" She shook her head. "Don't be silly, Luke, you're not forcing me to do dishes. I'm glad to help out. That's why I came in tonight after the get-together."

"I won't hear another word about it." Placing his palm

beneath her elbow, he led her away from the sink, gave her a dish towel to dry her hands, and guided her into the living room.

"Luke, honestly—"

"I'm starved," he said, changing the subject. "How 'bout you?"

"I'm—"

Before she could reply, he added, "I didn't eat much at the get-together tonight because I was too busy making sure the boys ate enough food. What do you say we order a pizza?" He picked up the phone book and leafed through it. "The boys will love cold pizza for lunch tomorrow."

Cici wrinkled her nose. She wasn't much for cold leftovers. Nevertheless, her stomach growled, and a hot, fresh pizza sounded marvelous.

"What do you like on your pie?"

"Just cheese and veggies. No meat."

Luke glanced at her with a twinkle in his eyes. "The movie made you hungry for vegetables, eh?"

She laughed in spite of herself and sat on the sofa. She listened as he ordered one "veggie delight" and one sausage and pepperoni.

"That's a lot of pizza," Cici remarked as Luke took his place in the armchair.

"My sons and I can down an entire pizza by ourselves."

"On second thought, that's not hard to believe." Tim, John, and Andy, a few of her guy friends, came to mind. They never seemed to fill up, especially when it came to junk food.

"So, tell me," Cici began, "how did you reprimand Aaron for his 'parachuting' tonight?"

"I just explained to him, again, about the possible catastrophes. For instance, if he lost his footing when he jumped, he could crash into the window and cut his arm. Then he'd need stitches and he might not be able to go swimming for weeks." Luke lazed back and crossed his legs. "Or, if he landed wrong, he could break his leg and he wouldn't be able to ride his bike or play outside for the rest of the summer."

She bobbed her head in understanding. "Teaching him to consider the consequences of his actions."

"Exactly. My kids aren't bad. They're just boys. And I'll admit that Aaron is my wild child, but I can reason with him—even at his young age. The other two are intent listeners so they learn from my explaining things to Aaron." Luke shrugged. "It works. At least it works for now."

"Good." Cici folded one leg beneath her and faced Luke. "Have you heard from Jen?"

"No. Have you heard from William?"

He shook his head.

Cici shrugged. "I don't expect we will, to tell you the truth. Jen is with the man she loves, and they're traipsing across Europe together with other friends. If it were me, I wouldn't give my friends back home a single thought."

Luke chuckled. "Maybe you're right. I remember feeling that way once." He seemed momentarily wistful, but then shook it off. He sucked in a breath and blew out a sigh. "After seeing Europe, William and Jen are scheduled to tour the Holy Lands. I'm envious."

It sounded as if Luke was envious of more than just Jen and William's trip abroad; however, she decided to avoid probing into his deep, innermost feelings. It wasn't her business anyway. "That's somewhere you'd like to visit? The Holy Lands?"

"For sure. It would be such a thrill to walk where Jesus did."

Cici stiffened. *Here it comes,* she thought. *He's going to question my beliefs and tell me why his are better.*

But to her surprise the conversation didn't stray in that direction.

"Have you done much traveling?"

Cici shook her head. "No. I've never left Iowa."

He laughed. "No kidding? How come?"

"Lack of funds." Cici felt herself relax since it appeared the topic of religion had been dropped. "Any extra money I earn has gone toward my education. It's been that way since

I graduated from high school. I worked my way through college, earned my degree, and now I'm about to earn my master's—that is, if I ever finish my thesis."

"And, as you mentioned, your research tonight has been for your thesis because it pertains to child development."

"Exactly." Cici was glad he'd brought up the subject of her thesis again. She never tired of discussing the topic.

"What about your family? Younger siblings? Nieces and nephews?"

"No. It's just my mom and me. My dad ran off with another woman when I was about twelve." A familiar bitterness mounted inside her. "After that, all my ideas about what a real family is evaporated into thin air. I learned early on to have a general distrust of men."

"I can relate. After my wife died, I went through a time where I had a general distrust of women. Sometimes I wonder if I still do."

"Oh?" This time Cici's curiosity got the better of her.

He sat forward. "Didn't William or Jen tell you about it?"

"About what?"

He regarded her with a thoughtful expression for several long moments. "My wife left a nightclub with some guy I'd never met or seen before. It may have been a lapse in judgment on her part, or she might have been having an affair with him. I guess I'll never know. She died in an accident that night. They were in his car, he was behind the wheel, and he died, too. He had no family in the area so they weren't much help in providing me with any clues. Thus my general distrust."

Cici hid her grimace. She couldn't imagine how painful the situation had to be for him. "I'm sorry. I had no idea."

He replied with a simple shrug. "I've had a lot of love and support from friends and family, and I muddled through the grief. I came to realize that I had to focus on the future and let God heal the past. I have three young boys to bring up. They depend on me."

"You must hate her."

"Who? My deceased wife?" Luke shook his head. "I could never hate Alissa. I loved her."

"You're serious, aren't you?"

Luke nodded. "Yes, I am."

Cici could tell he meant every word, and she was amazed that he didn't harbor any ill feelings for his departed wife. "Still, you must miss having a woman around—for your sons' sakes."

"Well, sure I do. I'm not as unfeeling as a streetlamp."

Cici grinned.

"This is a season, and God is aware and on top of my situation. He has my sons' best interests at heart, more than I ever could."

"I'm not sure about that, but you're right about everything being in constant change. The earth itself. . .life is cyclical. But without a mother figure in your sons' world, I can't help wondering who's going to hold them through all the disappointments in grade school? Who will nurture them into their adult years?"

A mischievous smirk pulled at the corner of his mouth. "Are you volunteering for the job?"

She rolled her eyes. "Of course not. I barely know you." She averted her gaze, willing away the memory of what took place in the kitchen just minutes ago. His touch affected her, and she hated to admit it.

He chuckled. "Seriously, God knows the future, and I trust Him to bring the right woman into our lives when He sees fit."

"Until then?"

"Until then, I'm a single dad."

"Well, that's where we differ. You see, my belief is that fathers can't nurture children the way mothers do. Women can single-handedly raise kids to become well-adjusted, productive citizens while men fall short of the mark time and time again."

Luke sat forward and placed his forearms on his knees. A

frown furrowed his dark brows. "How do you know?"

She leaned toward him. "I've done years of research on the subject of childrearing. My professor considers me an expert in the field."

"Well, I applaud you for all your work, but I think I can probably blow your research right out of the water."

"Oh?" Cici raised her brows and excitement pulsed through her veins at the sound of his challenge. "And how do you propose to do that?"

"See, my God is bigger than all the knowledge in the world. My God confounds even the wisest of men—and women."

"Please." Cici held up a forestalling hand, unimpressed. "Don't keep dragging God into this."

Luke sat back in silent acquiescence.

"On a human level, I still don't understand how you intend to prove me wrong. Especially when I intend to use you to prove my theory right."

"You intend to *use* me?" Luke seemed amused.

"I do, so consider yourself fairly warned."

"Okay. Then I'm going to pray that God will show you the truth about fathers raising their kids—and, yeah, I'm dragging God into this because He's in every part of my life. I'm going to trust that He'll show you that we, single dads, are equally as competent in every way as single moms."

Cici opened her mouth to retort, but the doorbell rang, cutting her off.

Luke stood and grinned. "Pizza's here."

five

Luke sat alone on his patio, enjoying a rare interval of peace. Several doors down, a neighbor's wind chimes tinkled in the breeze, and across the yard, on the adjacent property, some older kids laughed and splashed in an aboveground pool. Raucous sounds of summer—and, oddly, they helped Luke relax. He had tucked his boys into bed an hour ago, but the present respite was bittersweet since he'd had an extremely rough day. The boys had been at their naughtiest, and he hadn't gotten any work done in his office.

Lord, I'm praying that You'll show Ciara how I can be both a good father and mother. But the way I feel right now, I'd quit fatherhood if it were a regular paying job.

He sighed and allowed his thoughts to stray to his interim next-door neighbor. He liked her, from her curly auburn hair to her vivacious blue eyes and contagious smile. He wished she would have stayed longer last night, but she'd eaten one slice of pizza before leaving, saying she had more work to do on her thesis. While it irked him that she admitted to "using" him to prove her theory correct, her honesty was refreshing. He felt like he could let his guard down since her intentions were anything but romantic. Disappointing, yes, but he had no business romancing her anyway because she didn't share his faith. So, as far as he was concerned, she could bring on the research. Luke was confident in who he was: a Christian man who made his share of mistakes, but one who loved his children more than his own life.

Images of his sons scampered across his mind. Those little rascals—they'd been devilish today!

He released an audible sigh and shifted his weight in the lawn chair. Darkness was falling rapidly around him. Leaning his head back, he heard mosquitoes buzzing close to his ear, but he was too exhausted to even swat them away. He closed his eyes. . .

☙

Cici stepped out onto the patio for a quick breather. She inhaled deeply, allowing the cool night air to fill her lungs. Then she exhaled. After repeating the deep-breathing exercises several times, she felt the day's tension begin to seep from her body.

This morning she'd met with her professor, Agnes Carter-Hill, to talk about her thesis. Aggie was particularly interested in hearing about Cici's "living example" next door and encouraged further study. But she cautioned Cici not to get too personally involved.

How could I possibly get personally involved with Luke Weldon and his kids? First of all, he's not my type and secondly. . .

Her musings came to a halt at the sound of a man's light snoring on the other side of the fence. Her first thought was that someone's grandpa must be paying a visit next door, but when she peeked around the fence post she saw Luke sprawled out in a lawn chair, sleeping.

Cici swallowed a laugh and shook her head at the man. Then her smile slipped from her lips and a wave of empathy washed over her. Poor guy. He had his hands full with those three boys of his. Cici thought back on how exhausted she'd felt after eight hours working at a day care center. She could scarcely imagine how Luke managed 24/7 with his boys— and with his own business to run, also.

She stepped off the patio and onto the lush grass. She felt inexplicably drawn closer, as if she'd never seen a guy taking a catnap before. The university campus was littered with sleeping students at times. Still, she couldn't help wanting a better glimpse of him. As she crept closer, she saw his shadowed jaw beneath the moonlight. He wore jeans and a T-shirt. Cici watched his chest move slowly up and down with every snore.

She put her hand over her mouth, squelching a giggle. The sight of him seemed amusing and somehow endearing, as well.

Seconds later, a wail wafted through the second floor window. She froze and looked up at the house.

"Daddy. Daddy. . ."

One of the boys was crying. Probably one of the twins, Cici guessed. Casting aside all tentativeness, she strode toward Luke, placed her hand on his shoulder, and gave him a shake.

"Wake up, Luke."

He peeled open one eyelid. Seeing her, he bolted upright. "Ciara." He finger-combed his hair back off his forehead. "What's going on?"

He seemed embarrassed. "I hear one of the kids crying."

"Oh?" He pushed to his feet and they both listened.

It came again. "Daddy. Daddy. . ."

"You're right. Thanks for letting me know."

Concern made her follow him into the house. "Do you think he had a bad dream?"

"Not sure."

Cici trailed Luke up the steps. The layout of his condo was similar to Jen's next door, but the second floor had three bedrooms and a full bathroom.

At the doorway, Cici leaned against the wall and watched as Luke lifted the boy into his arms. "Is that Aaron?"

"Brian."

The boy whimpered.

"He's soaking wet. I think he's got a fever."

"What can I do to help?"

Luke carried the child out of the room, and Cici moved to close the door so as not to disturb the other boys. It was amazing they were still asleep.

"I'll get him out of his wet pajamas if you'll start a tepid bath for him."

"Tepid?" The word seemed so formal that it sounded odd coming from him, Mr. Laidback-and-casual.

"You know, lukewarm."

"Of course. . .sure. . ."

Cici hurried down the short hallway to the bathroom where she sat on the side of the tub and turned on the faucets. While waiting for the tub to fill, she took note of the net of plastic toys hanging from a corner hook. She also saw the dirty ring around the tub, and in that moment she realized Luke hadn't asked her in; she'd barged in and not for any sort of research, either. It's just that it had felt so natural.

Before she could dwell on it further, Luke entered the bathroom with Brian in his arms. She tested the bath. Its temperature definitely felt "tepid."

"It's full enough."

Cici shut off the water and stood to get out of his way.

"This isn't going to be pleasant." Luke's tone held a warning note while both worry and regret shone from his deep brown eyes. "He's burning up, and he's going to scream when I force him into this bath. Even though it's not cold, it'll feel like ice because his body temp is so high. But this is the only way I know to cool him down."

Cici paused to think it over. "What about a sponge bath?"

"Not as effective, but after Brian's bath I can use that as a means to keep him cool along with giving him children's acetaminophen."

Made sense to Cici. . .and she was rather impressed. Some fathers might call an ambulance or perhaps their mother, but Luke seemed confident in handling the situation. He'd likely taken care of plenty of fevers.

"Okay, well, what can I do next?"

"Would you mind going downstairs and getting the children's acetaminophen from the medicine shelf? It's on the very top shelf in one of the kitchen cupboards—same cupboard as the drinking glasses."

"Sure."

Cici left the bathroom and closed the door behind her. Then, just as Luke predicted, Brian let out an ear-piercing shriek. Cici's heart broke. A lukewarm bath could feel like torture when a body felt as hot as a charcoal grill. But she reminded herself that the alternative was the fever continuing to rage and Brian possibly suffering a convulsion—or worse.

She found the medicine and made her way back upstairs. The screaming had stopped and only Brian's soft whines and whimpers came from behind the bathroom door.

Minutes passed, and finally Luke appeared with his son wrapped in a towel.

"Hi, Miss Ciara." Even as sick as he was, the little guy managed a weak smile for her benefit.

She was touched to the heart by his sweet gesture.

Once Brian was clad in clean, lightweight pajamas, Cici handed the medicine to Luke and he administered it. Then they went into the living room downstairs where Luke settled the little guy on the couch before turning on the TV.

"Can I sit next to you?" Cici asked.

Brian nodded. "And my dad can sit here." He patted the cushion to his left.

Cici made herself comfortable. "Does anything hurt? Your throat or your ears?"

The boy shook his head. "I feel all better now." He scratched his tummy and then the back of his neck.

Luke sat down and released a long, weary sigh.

"Long day, huh, Superman?" Cici couldn't resist the urge to tease him.

"You can say that again." He sent her a dubious glance. "Something tells me I'll get no sympathy from you."

"Au contraire." She continued to smile. "I sympathize. I worked in children's day care, remember?" She grew serious. "That's why I barged in again tonight. I thought I could be of some help."

Luke stretched. "You did barge in again, didn't you?"

Cici grinned at the comeback. *"Touché."*

He chuckled. "Oh, and speaking of. . .your use of the French language reminds me of the e-mail William sent. I read it this morning. He and Jen are fine and having a great time touring Paris."

"I'm so jealous."

"Daddy, itch my back." A frown pinched Brian's features while he wiggled to alleviate the discomfort.

Luke gave him an accommodating scratch and glanced at the TV before looking back at Cici. "Are you jealous because you didn't get an e-mail or because you're not in Paris?"

"Both." Cici smiled, knowing she didn't begrudge either William or Jen an ounce of happiness. She only wished she were done with her master's degree, had a great-paying job, and could enjoy a trip abroad. "I'll get over it."

"Daddy, now I'm itchy all over."

Cici stared at the little boy beside her and noticed the pink spots that had seemingly appeared out of nowhere.

"Uh-oh." Cici peered at Luke, wide-eyed.

He inspected Brian's face, arms, and back before expelling an audible sigh as he met her gaze. "A couple of days ago, I thought these were bug bites, but, um. . ." He cleared his throat. "I hope you've had the chicken pox. Looks just like 'em, from what I remember when a friend's kids came down with the virus."

She nodded. "I had the chicken pox as a kid." She tipped her head. "And you?"

"Yeah, I'm pretty sure I did, too." He turned his attention back to Brian. "I had planned to call the doctor in the morning anyway."

"If I'm not mistaken, the county will send over a visiting nurse so you won't have to bring Brian into the office and contaminate others."

"I think you're right."

She nodded. "And I think your future is going to hold giving Brian plenty of oatmeal baths and applying calamine lotion, although I'm sure the nurse will instruct you how to treat chicken pox."

Luke groaned and flopped back against the couch cushions.

"Daddy, is chicken pox those round things you put in the oven and when they're all done we turn 'em upside down on a plate and eat 'em?"

"What?" Luke frowned, obviously trying to interpret. Then his eyes lit up with understanding. "You're talking about chicken pot pies and, no, chicken pox is different." He chuckled. "Come on. I'll show you what chicken pox looks like in the bathroom mirror."

Luke stood and took Brian into the downstairs powder room, and Cici decided she'd leave. She had left the back door unlocked since she hadn't planned on going any farther than the patio.

"I'll see you later, Luke," she called as she made her way through the kitchen. As usual, the room was in disarray. Dirty dishes filled the sink, and unwashed pots and pans stood on the stove. One seemed to have been used to cook scrambled eggs and the other to heat canned corn.

Was that dinner tonight? After eating cold pizza for breakfast and who-knows-what for lunch, those kids had scrambled eggs and canned corn for dinner?

Cici wrinkled her nose. Those were hardly the meals she'd serve her children. Seconds later, she recalled hearing of worse meals dads made for their kids. She'd read reports in which some fathers never even bothered to feed their children so they either starved or learned to steal.

She paused, surveyed the mess, and debated whether to stay and help clean up.

"Don't even think about it."

Pivoting, she smiled at Luke. "You're a mind reader now?"

He laughed. "Yeah, well, you know. . .us superheroes. . ."

Cici rolled her eyes.

"Seriously, it'll take me fifteen minutes to clean this place up. But I appreciate your willingness to help."

"Sure. Anytime." She strode toward the back door.

"And, Ciara?"

Once again, she stopped and turned to face him.

"Thanks for lending me a hand tonight with Brian."

"No problem."

She met his gaze and saw his earnest expression. What's more, she felt the fascinating kinetics between them again.

"Call me Cici. My friends do."

"I think Ciara suits you."

She laughed. "I don't know about that. My mom named me after her favorite perfume." With a smile still on her face, she regarded him, noting the intensity in his brown eyes. She felt both embarrassed and flattered by his remark.

"If you don't mind, I'd prefer to call you Ciara. It's a beautiful name." Luke's voice was but a whisper. "You're beautiful, too."

She'd never had anyone say that to her before. "What a sweet thing to say, Luke." The attraction she felt toward him escalated. "I admire sensitivity in a man."

A hint of a smile tugged at his mouth.

She moved toward him with slow, deliberate steps, wondering what it would feel like to linger in his arms and kiss him. Instincts told her that he'd like to find out, too.

But just as she reached him with the intention of slipping her arms around his neck and urging his lips to hers, Brian padded down the vinyl floor of the hall.

"Daddy, are Devin and Aaron gonna get chicken pies, too?"

"Um. . ." Luke blinked and turned to his son.

The magic of the moment vanished.

"I think they probably will," he answered. He cleared his throat as if clearing his mind, also.

Likewise, reality rattled Cici to her core. She couldn't believe what she'd been thinking.

She took two steps backward. "I'll be leaving now. . ."

Luke looked at her with an expression of remorse. Was he sorry she didn't kiss him? Or was he sorry she'd attempted?

With a parting smile, Cici left and trotted next door. She felt overwhelmed and awed by what just took place. Entering her kitchen, she closed the door to the patio and leaned against it. Her professor's warning not to get personally involved rang in her ears. Again she wondered at those fleeting seconds of what had to be sheer insanity.

Just then a shadow moved across the walls between the kitchen and living room. Cici's heart began to hammer when she realized she was about to face an intruder. But before she could react, Chase Tibbits stepped into view. His bulky frame filled the archway.

"Hey," he said in a booming voice, "you should never leave your doors wide open. Never know who might get in."

six

"Get out, Chase!"

He stepped closer, and Cici sensed he'd been drinking. He smelled as rancid as spilled beer on a barstool.

"Hey, now don't get your dander up. I rang the bell before I walked in."

Cici narrowed her gaze and put her hands on her hips, hoping she appeared formidable. In truth, she'd never felt more vulnerable in her life.

"Quit glaring at me like that."

"Get out!"

"Look, I was just being neighborly." He swaggered slightly. "I got worried. I thought maybe you were laying dead somewhere in here so I came around back to check on you. Door wasn't locked."

"Chase, if you don't leave, I'm calling the police." Fear caused her voice to tremble, but she didn't think he noticed. "Now, get out!"

The threat of the cops didn't seem to faze him. "Tori said you're working on some report about kids and dads. I got a boy, almost eight years old, and you can study me and him all you want."

Cici tamped down her panic. The man stood over six feet and probably weighed more than two fifty. There was no way she could fight him and win. "I want you to leave, Chase."

He seemed to ignore her. "My ex-wife spoils the kid rotten, but whenever he's with me he doesn't get away with a single thing."

"Seriously. Get out before I call the cops." She snatched Jen's cordless phone off the kitchen counter.

"All right, all right. I'm leaving." He turned around, and,

without further comment or complaint, let himself out the front entrance.

Relieved, Cici rushed into the living room and locked the door behind him. As she turned the dead bolt, the back doorbell rang and she heard Luke calling her name. No doubt he'd heard the commotion.

"Coming." She hurried to the back door.

"Everything all right?" Luke's voice came through the aluminum screen door. "I don't mean to be nosy, but I heard raised voices, and—"

"Everything's fine." Setting down the phone, she hugged herself, feeling more troubled by Chase's intrusion than she cared to admit. How rude of him to just walk in and lurk around! She wondered if he'd stolen anything.

"You sure you're okay?"

She heard the concern in Luke's tone and gulped down the sudden knot in her throat before bobbing her head in reply. Next she opened her mouth to tell Luke what had happened, but it occurred to her that he was one of two men who had evoked intense emotions in her tonight. Cici prided herself on her even temperament, her levelheadedness.

"Ciara, what in the world is going on?"

"Good question." She forced a smile and felt her composure returning. "Seriously, I'm fine. I just had a bit of a scare. Chase Tibbits was here. He got in because I left the back door unlocked while I was over at your place, helping with Brian."

"Chase? Inside your place? You're not serious?" Before she could stop him, he opened the screen door and stepped into the kitchen. "Is he still here?"

"He's gone," she said as Luke marched into the living room, looking around. "I'm really all right. It was kind of you to come over, though."

"Chase really came in—and stayed here—knowing you weren't home?" Luke stopped in front of her and stood with his arms akimbo. "I think we should inform the police."

Cici picked up on the word "we." It warmed her heart to

think he was willing to adopt her problem. Nevertheless, she shook her head in reply. "Maybe he was only here for two or three minutes before I walked in. Let's just forget it." She kept her eyes averted, fearing her emotions might overtake her common sense again and she'd land in Luke's arms one way or another. "I think Chase was drinking tonight. I'm almost certain he didn't mean to alarm me, even though he did."

"Okay, we won't call the cops. It's your decision. But you can always change your mind and file a complaint tomorrow."

"I know. Thanks."

She finally lifted her gaze, noticing—not for the first time—the strong set to Luke's whiskered jaw. Her gaze traveled up his face and she recognized a light of interest shining in his cocoa brown eyes.

Before her senses reeled for the second time, she moved away. How odd and disconcerting that she should feel attracted to a guy like Luke. Only a month ago she would have laughed at the mere suggestion. A software designer? A Christian? No way. She'd prefer a more intellectual, academic type—if and when that time came.

"You'd better get back home. Brian might need you."

"He's sound asleep." He pulled a monitor from his pocket and held it up.

"Well, just the same. . ." Couldn't he see she was grappling with her emotions? "I, um, should really get back to work on my thesis."

He inclined his head. "But before I go, let me leave my phone number. . .just in case."

She found a slip of paper and a pen. He scribbled down the information.

"Thanks."

"I'm serious. Call if you need me."

Cici was touched by his offer, which somehow only heightened her tumultuous feelings. "Good night, Luke."

"Good night."

She watched him leave and, after he was gone, she closed

the door and turned the lock. Suddenly she could breathe again.

Crazy night.

She had to regroup. Get her thoughts back in line. Using a relaxation technique she'd learned in a yoga class years ago, Cici tried to free her mind and rid her body of its tension. Her thoughts came around to her best friend, and a grin tugged at her mouth; Jen could have warned her that there were two dangerous men in the neighborhood: an unpredictable lout and a Christian superhero with three rambunctious but adorable sons.

❧

Almost two weeks later, Luke found himself awake at dawn. In the rare moments of quiet, his thoughts wandered to a certain redhead next door. She'd been an invaluable help to him in recent days since the boys got sick. All three had come down with the chicken pox almost simultaneously. Turns out a neighbor kid had the virus and passed it along. Church friends and family members offered their assistance, too, but Luke found it was Ciara he looked forward to seeing every day.

But I shouldn't. She's not a believer.

His heart and conscience battled.

But she's helping me with the kids, and I'm totally in control of my emotions. Sure, I've wanted to kiss her. I'll admit it. Except I haven't. And Ciara has been nothing but polite.

Luke shifted. His body teetered on the edge of the bed as his sons, one by one, had climbed in with him sometime during the night. Unable to sleep, he stood and pulled on some clothes before tiptoeing from his room. He made his way downstairs to the kitchen, yawning as he scooped freshly ground coffee into a filter. He put it into the coffeemaker and, once the java was brewing, he strode to the window and peered outside. A golden hue illuminated the horizon, promising another gorgeous summer day. Maybe he'd allow the boys some outdoor playtime, although the nurse who'd visited warned him that, like with any virus, the kids needed to rest. However, they were feeling pent up and somewhat stir-crazy—and so was Luke.

Lord, this is the day You have made. I will rejoice and be glad in it—even though I've got three kids with chicken pox and a business to run.

Once more, he thought of Ciara's visits in past days. She played with the boys, read to them—when they could sit still long enough to listen to a story—and she gave Luke a break so he could get a little work done in his home office. Neighbors, friends, and family members came and went, offering their assistance, too, and bringing over meals. At times, Luke's front entrance seemed like a revolving door. But those folks, as thoughtful and kindhearted as they were, seemed more like company paying visits. When Ciara came by, he didn't too much care if the dishes were in the sink or the laundry basket sat in the middle of the living room. She'd seen the mess before and hadn't taken offense. A certain comfort level had been established between them, and yet a certain level of caution had developed, too. It was as if they were both battling the inevitable and, in Luke's case, the forbidden.

Lord, the last thing I need in my life is a woman who doesn't share my faith. It was heartache enough for me when Alissa abandoned her beliefs for what she thought was a good time with her friends. . .and maybe even another man.

The timer on the coffeemaker sounded and Luke shook himself. He turned from the window and walked to the cupboard where he pulled a mug from the shelf and filled it with the strong-smelling, steamy brew. Coffee in hand, he retrieved the morning newspaper from the front step. The breeze that met him smelled sweet and fresh, like dew on an Iowa cornfield, and Luke filled his lungs with early morning air.

Stepping outside, he left the front door ajar in case the kids woke up, then he lowered himself onto the cement stoop. The neighborhood was quiet except for the occasional car or pickup truck that passed on the otherwise deserted street, so Luke decided to continue his heart-to-heart chat with the Lord.

There are a lot of good qualities about Ciara. She's a very giving person. She likes to help people and she knows I'm grateful for the times she's dropped in and lent me a hand. The kids like her. . .

Someone honked and Luke startled. He recognized Tori Evenrod and waved as she zoomed off in her yellow convertible. He had to grin at the woman's pluck and flamboyance.

Ciara's got a lot of gumption, too. She's goal-oriented and determined. What's more, she seems like a loyal person.

God's still, small voice seemed to reply: *"Do not be yoked together with unbelievers. . .what fellowship can light have with darkness?"*

Reality check.

Luke drew in a deep breath just as he heard a door open and close next door. He glanced over in time to see Ciara step onto the front walk.

"G'morning."

She turned with a start, and her hand fluttered to the base of her throat.

Luke grimaced. "Didn't mean to scare you. Sorry."

She relaxed visibly. "Guess I spook easily ever since *you know who* paid me that surprise visit a couple of weeks ago."

Luke nodded. He knew she referred to the night she found Chase roaming around inside Jen's condo.

A moment passed, and he couldn't help noticing how her outfit accentuated the fact that she had curves in all the right places. A stretchy, sleeveless, multicolored, striped tank over snug-fitting faded jeans. He then saw the brown leather sandals on her feet with her polished pink toenails peeping out the front. Lifting his gaze, he pushed out an embarrassed little smile and tried not to admit he liked what he saw. Instead he took a gulp of his coffee and watched as she hiked the strap of her pink and black leather computer bag higher onto her freckled shoulder. Her blue eyes shifted from his face to the cup in his hands and Luke remembered his manners.

"Would you like some coffee? I've got plenty."

"No, thanks. I need to be on my way."

He inclined his head. "Well, have a good one."

"I'll try, but I have an appointment with my professor, and she's not going to be pleased that I'll be late handing in my thesis."

Luke sent her a sympathetic wince.

"But then I'm meeting some friends for lunch, so I have that to look forward to."

"Sounds like fun." He took another swallow of coffee.

"Yeah, should be. Have a good day, yourself."

"Thanks. I will."

Ciara smiled and strode to her car.

Luke watched her go and wondered how to proceed. On one hand he wanted to be a good testimony of God's love and goodness. He also relished the times when Ciara came over and helped with the kids. On the other, he couldn't deny his attraction to her. Could he continue operating in the middle of the road, so to speak? Riding the fence? Wrestling with temptation—and winning?

He reminded himself that with God all things are possible.

After raking a hand through his hair, he relaxed and finished his coffee. Pushing to his feet, he went back inside to open his Bible and see what God had to say to him this morning.

seven

"Are you losing your focus?"

"I—I don't know," Cici stammered, watching Professor Agnes Carter-Hill fold her hands while she sat behind the steel-gray desk. Shelves packed with books lined the entire wall behind her. Some of the titles in her vast collection included *Spock Rocks!*, *Village Parenting*, *Woman and Child*, *Females In The Mother/Father Roles*, and *A Happy Home Without Dads*. Cici had read a number of Aggie's precious volumes and, because of her own upbringing, she could relate to them on several different levels; however, of late, Luke Weldon had somehow proved each study and theory to be little more than ridiculous fabrications.

"You know," Aggie said, drawing Cici from her musings, "there's a good chance our work will be used in the State Supreme Court as evidence to support new rulings. I've documented case upon case in both my master's thesis and my doctorate dissertation, and I've taught you to do the same." A proud smile split her face and dozens of soft wrinkles appeared around her eyes and mouth. Cici was always reminded of the binding of a well-loved book whenever Aggie looked pleased, laughed, or smiled. "Do you realize that we could have a hand in changing the face of the American family as we know it?" Leaning back in her leather desk chair, Aggie raised her arms in victory. "What a boon for women everywhere in this country!"

Cici smiled, thinking her mother would be so proud. Ever since Cici was in junior high school, Mom had been forced to be both mother and father in her life. It had been difficult economically, but Mom did the best she could. Today she and Cici were successful women, despite having no men in their lives. Aggie was right: They didn't need men. But this wasn't just about single women; it was about children's welfare and what was best for them. As for those Weldon boys, Cici admitted they certainly needed their daddy, and Luke was great with them. True, she had first assumed he was a Peter Pan example for his children, but now she thought it was a beautiful thing, watching him and his young sons interact. Luke was kind yet firm, playful, but maintained proper boundaries.

Cici stifled a sigh. And whenever Luke looked at her with those penetrating coffee-colored eyes of his, her legs felt like linguini.

"You're exhausted. I can tell." Aggie sat forward. "Okay, listen, I'll grant you an extension. Your thesis must be in my office by September first. But that's it. No more extensions."

Cici stood and nodded. "You got it." She forced a smile as a skeptical feeling oozed through her. She'd had every intention of finishing her thesis by August, but now even the September extension didn't sound like enough time. Her thoughts were so jangled. "Thanks for understanding, Aggie, and I'll try not to disappoint."

The professor nodded, sending the reading glasses perched atop her head tumbling onto the desk. "I know you won't." She smoothed back her short, straight, dark hair. "I've mentored you to the best of my academic and personal abilities, and I expect a masterpiece."

Again, Cici pushed out a smile as her confidence dwindled all the more.

Leaving her professor's office, Cici made her way down the empty corridor. The soles of her sandals clapped against the polished marble floor and echoed around her. Not many people were on campus in early July. The six-week long summer session had just ended, and now practically everyone was gearing up and making plans for the Fourth of July holiday. Since the holiday fell on a Friday, most were making a long weekend of it.

Everyone but Cici. She was determined to hole up in Jen's office and work through the holiday weekend. No parties. No movies. No phone calls. No e-mails. And especially no distractions from her handsome neighbor next door.

Except Cici had a hunch that avoiding Luke and his kids might teeter on the impossible. The boys were just getting over the chicken pox, and Luke had his hands full. Cici knew he appreciated the help she gave him—and she enjoyed it. The only trouble was, Luke had messed up her thinking. They'd never debated any political or spiritual issues. They never discussed controversial matters. He kept his word and respected her beliefs, but he lived out his own and everything he did brought back snippets of conversations Cici'd had in the past with Jen and William. In essence, Luke was proving that everything they told her was true, and Cici was both curious and confused by this unexpected turn of events. What's more, her thesis statement had become skewed in a way that seemed irreparable; however, she didn't dare tell Aggie. The woman was a diehard feminist, and Cici had believed she was heading in the same direction until she met Luke. Now, suddenly, her entire world seemed to have been knocked off its axis.

Cici exited the building and walked across the sparsely populated lot on the university campus and climbed into her car. Key in the ignition, she started the engine and drove the short distance to the restaurant where she'd planned to meet her two college roommates, Bridget and Tanya, for lunch. She parked, entered the establishment, and found the two blonds sitting at a table near the bar area. The young women saw her approaching and stood.

"Hi!" Cici hugged first Tanya and then Bridget. "What's new with you two?"

"Nothing much." Bridget lowered herself back into her wooden chair. "Same ol' thing."

Cici looked at Tanya. "What about you?"

"Oh. . ." Tanya's expression fell. "I broke up with Ryan."

"Sorry to hear that, although it was a long time coming. Wasn't it?"

"Yes, but I really believed Ryan was the guy for me." Tears filled Tanya's hazel eyes.

"Is reconciliation a possibility?"

"Not now, not while he's got a drinking problem." Bridget answered for Tanya, studying her brokenhearted friend as she blinked away her tears. "Tanya realized, and rightly so, that Ryan needs some help before he can be in a healthy relationship."

"It's a good thing I found out before I did something stupid like marry the guy." Tanya's gaze dropped to the cola in front of her. "So much for earning my *M-R-S* degree this year."

Cici grinned at her flaxen-haired friend. "At least you've still got your sense of humor."

Tanya lifted her chin and looked across the table at her. "I'm serious. I want to get married and be a wife and a mommy."

Cici coveted a mommy role in the future, too, but she shook her head at the wifely part of the statement. "You should want to build a successful career for yourself. Don't give everything up for a man."

"Careers can come and go, Ceece, but I was always taught that love never fails. And if you were perfectly honest, you'd admit that you'd ditch that women's lib stuff if the right guy came along."

"I'll admit to no such thing." Cici gave each friend an exasperated glance. "Building your lives around men will only lead to the same anguish that Tanya is experiencing now. However, if a woman is educated and continues to learn and grow as an individual, she will always have a safety net in which to fall if the opportunity for marriage doesn't present itself—or if her husband dumps her for another woman like my dad left my mother."

"I'm all about those safety nets." Tanya sipped her cola.

The server came and took their lunch orders then fetched Cici an iced tea.

"So, speaking of men, how's your love life?" Bridget donned an impish grin. "Boring as ever?"

"I'm on a sabbatical and writing my master's thesis. I'm not supposed to have a love life right now."

Her roommates looked at each other. "Boring as ever," they said in unison.

"That's what you think." The words spewed out before Cici could swallow them down.

"You met someone?" Bridget leaned forward, wearing an interested expression.

"Sort of. He just lives next door to Jen and. . .he's single with three little boys." She muttered the latter while placing the napkin in her lap, wishing she'd never said a word.

"How'd you meet him?"

"Who is he?"

"Handsome? Good job?"

"Jen's neighbor? Unbelievable!" Bridget sat back in awe. "What's his name?"

"Whoa!" Cici held up her hands as if to shield herself from the questions they hurled at her. "Like I said, he's Jen's neighbor, and he knows her and William." She paused, hoping the association would set in. When two pairs of eyes just stared back at her, she added what should have been obvious. "He's a Christian. He doesn't drink, smoke, party, or swear. He pretty much works at his home-based business, takes care of his kids, and goes to church."

"Can I have his phone number?" A dreamy smile curled Bridget's full lips. "I'd love to date a guy who's just plain ol' nice, you know?"

"Yeah, I know. I recently broke up with a drunk who had violent tendencies." Tanya glanced at Bridget before looking back at Cici. "Does this neighbor guy of yours have a friend?"

Sitting back in her chair, Cici felt stunned. "What? The party girls would rather date a Christian than one of their 'cool dude' acquaintances? I don't believe it."

"I'm burned out." With the admission Tanya's expression fell.

Bridget agreed. "I guess we learned the hard way that it's better to leave the party early than to stay and ruin your entire life."

"Jen's a great example of that," Tanya pointed out. "She straightened up her life, finished school, met a nice guy, and now she's getting married in October. I'm so happy for her."

Cici was more than amazed by what she was hearing. This certainly didn't sound like the same Tanya and Bridget she'd been rooming with. In fact, her two party-hearty roomies were the reason she'd moved into Jen's place. She knew she'd never find a moment's peace with all their friends coming and going. In the past, Cici hadn't cared since she wasn't home a lot. But in order to write a thesis, one needed solitude and an ambiance that promoted intellect. . .

Which, she realized, didn't exactly describe her present situation, either—not with those noisy superheroes next door.

"Hey, what do you hear from Jen, anyway?" Tanya sat forward, looking eager. "How's her trip going? Must be so romantic to tour Europe with the man you love."

"I want to hear more about Jen's next-door neighbor." A teasing grin played across Bridget's pink lips.

The food arrived and the easy banter continued. Cici hadn't planned to talk about Luke, but her friends managed to pry information out of her anyway.

"So, you see, the entire situation is so confusing, not to mention distracting." Cici picked at her seafood salad and finally popped a piece of tomato into her mouth. "I set out to prove my thesis using Luke as a prime example of an inconsequential father figure, but he seems to be proving me wrong and it's messing up my head."

"Is this the first time you've been in love?" Tanya asked between bites of her BLT sandwich.

"In love?" Cici brought her chin back. "I'm not in love.

I'm just. . .attracted to him in a curious sort of way because he's so opposite of me and everything I've worked so hard to become."

"Hold it. You met a man who can make you pull your head out of your books and you're not in love?" Bridget chuckled. "You deceive yourself, Miss Academia."

Cici narrowed her gaze. "Very funny."

Bridget and Tanya both wore amused little smirks.

"How does he feel about you?"

Cici replied with a quick shrug. "My guess is he's interested in me, too, although he doesn't give in to his emotions. I don't know if he's just extremely polite or if I'm misreading his body language."

"Maybe he thinks it's a sin if he kisses you." Tanya pointed at her with a long French fry. "I knew a guy in high school like that."

"But we're adults." Cici didn't think that was the case at all. "Besides, I saw Jen kiss William, so it can't be that great of a sin."

"Listen, I went to a religious private high school." Bridget's voice held an authoritative note. "Intimacy before marriage is a huge no-no. It's in the Bible and everything, except don't ask me where because I never paid attention in our religion classes."

"Figures," Tanya quipped.

Cici forked another bite of her salad into her mouth and mulled over the last bit of their conversation. "I never imagined I'd be attracted to a Christian man, even though Jen's my best friend."

"But you and Jen have been friends for years," Bridget pointed out. "Would you be close to her at this point in your life if you just met Jen today, knowing she's got religion and you don't?"

The question gave Cici pause.

"To tell you the truth, I'm envious of Jen," Tanya said. "I'd rather date a Christian man than an alcoholic any day. I feel like I'm emerging from a nightmare because of everything I went through with Ryan."

Bridget reached over and clasped Tanya's hand. "You'll get over it. You did the right thing in breaking off your relationship with him."

Cici saw tears form in her friend's eyes and her heart ached. Then, suddenly the image of Chase Tibbits, intoxicated and wandering around Jen's living room uninvited, flashed through Cici's mind. His drunken presence had scared the wits out of her, and Cici was forced to agree with Tanya: She'd rather date a Christian than a problem drinker, too.

"Well, in my humble opinion, the game of love boils down to nothing more than chemistry between two people. It's all about the chemistry." Bridget took a drink of her cola. "It's either there or it's not."

Cici's insides turned warm and fluttery. She had felt that indescribable existential force between herself and Luke more times than she cared to count—every time she saw him, in fact.

"Look," she said, wondering whom she hoped to convince, her friends or herself, "whatever I'm feeling for Luke will pass soon enough. I've got a new deadline for my thesis, and I've got to concentrate on finishing it."

"Good luck." Tanya smiled. "Your heart might just overrule your common sense."

The reply rang loudly in Cici's head, like church bells on Sunday morning.

Or was it really some sort of knell?

eight

A brilliant sunset blazed on the horizon as Cici climbed out of her car. She'd spent hours talking with her friends and catching up on their lives before going to the library where she wrote several pages of her thesis. Her resolve returned once she concluded that she could present a more objective point of view and still prove her theory. According to her research, Luke's fathering skills were an exception and not the norm. Besides, he had the support of his church, which was more assistance than many single mothers received.

Cici ambled up the walkway and unlocked the condo door. She entered and deposited her laptop on the living room table, determined to immediately start working on her thesis again. But as she settled into the sofa and booted up her computer, she heard wails coming from next door. She couldn't help but wonder what was going on. Was Aaron in trouble again? Or one of the boys ill and miserable?

In spite of herself, she made her way to the Weldons' to see if she could help. Surprisingly, she found Luke on his patio, barbecuing on the outdoor grill.

"Hi, Ciara." He barely looked up from the wieners he was cooking.

"I can hear one of the kids crying, so I thought I'd come over to see if I might lend a helping hand."

"Thanks, but I can manage."

Cici thought the muttered reply sounded a bit short. "Bad day?"

"The worst."

She pressed her lips together to keep from smiling, not at the fact that Luke had a tough time today, but how quickly he admitted to it. That said a lot in her estimation.

She eyed the smoking grill. "Whacha burning?"

"Supper."

On tiptoes she peeked over his shoulder. "I don't think those hot dogs can get much blacker."

"The boys like 'em well done."

"That's good." She lifted the white plastic plate from off the grill's wooden rack. "I'd say they're as well done as they'll get."

She held the plate in his direction and, using the pair of tongs in his hand, he removed the charred wieners from the open flames.

"Why don't you take a break, Luke? I'll feed the boys."

He raked his fingers through his walnut brown hair and looked off in the distance for several moments before bringing his gaze back to her. "This'll be great for your thesis, won't it? The helpless dad who can't even get his kids fed because of all the chaos in his home?"

"What?" His question surprised her.

Luke had the good grace to look contrite. "I'm sorry. My remark was harsh. But you know what I mean. My present situation is a perfect example of why you think a single dad can't raise his kids."

"Well, to be honest, I'd normally agree with you, but considering the fact that your sons have had the chicken pox and you're obviously exhausted, let's just forget it. This is off the record. Just one neighbor helping another."

Luke half shrugged, half nodded.

Cici grinned. He resembled one of his little guys just now. "Cheer up, okay? If it's any consolation, even single moms have bad days."

"I'm sure they do."

"They do. Trust me. My mom had plenty of them. So relax for a while. I'm happy to help out." She walked into his kitchen and Luke didn't try to stop her.

Devin and Brian sat at the table, looking forlorn. Their faces were covered with scabby red dots.

"Hi, superheroes." Cici smiled.

Their countenances brightened just a little.

"Where's Aaron?"

"He was bad," Devin informed her. "So he's upstairs."

That explained the crying she'd heard minutes ago.

Moving farther into the kitchen, Cici spied an empty can on the counter and the baked beans in a saucepan on the stove. She presumed the syrupy legumes were part of the supper plan, too. The boys confirmed it and then instructed her as to how they liked their hot dogs prepared—lots of ketchup, no mustard. Once they were eating, Cici fetched Aaron. He was in the bedroom he shared with his brothers, lying on the upper bunk, sobbing. A few soft words, however, and his tears dissipated. By the time she'd led him down to the kitchen, his mood had lifted and a "cowboy dinner" appealed to him.

As she sat at the round kitchen table, watching the children eating, Cici had to grin at the term "cowboy dinner." She supposed superheroes could deign to eat wieners and baked beans.

She glanced toward the screen door and caught a glimpse of Luke reclining in one of the lawn chairs on the patio, his face tilted toward the late afternoon sun. He appeared completely exhausted, and she wished she could do more to help him out.

She gazed back at the boys, and an idea began to form. She stood. "I'll be right back, guys. Okay?"

Their heads bobbed in unison and Cici noticed the sugary syrup and ketchup collecting around their lips as they chewed.

She smiled at the sight of the boys enjoying their food and walked outside. Reaching Luke, she touched him on the shoulder. He jumped to attention.

"I didn't mean to startle you."

"No problem. I must have dozed off." He rubbed one eye and then the other. "Sorry 'bout that."

"No need to be sorry." Cici's heart went out to her bedraggled neighbor. "Listen, I'd like to take the boys out for ice cream. May I?"

"Uh…" Luke hedged.

"It'll give you time to regroup, and I promise to keep the kids away from other people so they don't share their chicken pox."

He smiled. "I'd love the break, and they're probably not contagious anymore; their spots have scabbed over." He raked his fingers through his hair, appearing pensive for a good fifteen seconds. "They only look frightening, but they've all had temperaments to match."

"I imagine they're tired of being cooped up."

Luke bobbed his head in agreement. "I figured by the Fourth of July they'll feel—*and look*—like themselves again and we can enjoy the holiday."

"That's only two days away." Cici wondered what sort of plans Luke had made. Part of her wished he'd ask her to join him and the boys, but her thesis awaited. "So what do you say? Can I take the kids out for ice cream tonight?"

"They're a handful."

"I think I can manage."

"Okay. . .yeah, sure."

In spite of his amiable smile, Cici thought his attitude was somewhat brusque. She'd noticed it before, too. Still, she knew Luke trusted her, otherwise he wouldn't allow her to take the boys for ice cream. However, she couldn't quite understand his aloofness.

Or was it that he didn't want her to go?

Cici dashed the notion. Luke was just tired, that's all.

She re-entered the kitchen and, after the boys finished eating, she told them her plans to take them for ice cream. She laughed when they clambered off their chairs and jumped up and down, cheering all the while.

Luke held out his keys. "I think it'd be easier if you take my minivan. The twins' car seats and Devin's booster seat are secured in there, and I'd hate to have to transfer them."

Cici reached out and slowly accepted the proffered keys. She hadn't thought about car seats.

Embarrassment filled her. Here she was supposed to be an expert on children! "Thanks."

"Well, it's the least I can do." He spoke loudly in order to be heard above his children's excited voices.

"Can we go now?"

"I want cookie dough ice cream."

"When are we leaving?"

"Right away." Cici surveyed the upturned faces and eager brown eyes staring at her. "I just need to grab my purse and lock up next door."

"Hurry, okay?"

"Devin, remember your manners." Luke's tone held a parental warning. He turned to Cici. "We'll meet you by the garage in front."

"Sounds good."

Once again, she sensed the terseness behind the words he spoke. As she made her way back into Jen's condo, she decided Luke was certainly in one cranky mood this evening.

&

Feeling like he needed some adult companionship, Luke phoned a couple of his buddies and asked them to stop by. Within twenty minutes both Jesse and Trevor were sitting in his living room, lending sympathetic ears.

"There's no way I can avoid her. She's renting Jen Hargrove's condo next door. And today I had a really bad day with the boys until she showed up like a godsend, fed the kids, and took them out for ice cream. She enjoys helping me out and the kids adore her." Luke hesitated before admitting the rest. "I'm beginning to adore her, too."

"Hmm, I see the dilemma." Jesse nodded while a concerned frown pulled at his thick, blond brows. "She's not a believer, but the attraction's there."

"Why don't you just come out and tell her about your faith, your feelings for her," Trevor said, "and explain that it's impossible for you to give in to your emotions and please God, too?"

Luke considered his friend's suggestion, thinking that "Blunt" had to be the guy's middle name. "I don't want to turn her off of Christianity."

"William and Jen evidently haven't turned her off and they're pretty straightforward." Trevor lifted a can of cola to his mouth and took a swig.

"I suppose that's true enough."

"That's one way to handle it." Jesse sat forward on the sofa. "But I wasn't a Christian until I met Mandy. We worked in an office together and when I finally asked her out to dinner, she accepted the invite. I knew she was different than other women I'd gone out with, and she talked about her faith in God. But she never once snubbed me or said she couldn't date me. I grew more and more curious about her and when I realized I was in love with her, I decided to tag along to church because I knew it was important to her. Wasn't long before God got a hold of my heart, and I made the decision to become a Christian, too."

"So you're telling me to trust God and let my relationship with Ciara develop?" Luke pondered the idea. It appealed to him, of course—although he'd never been an advocate of "dating evangelism." Then again, Alissa had claimed to be a believer, and her life had ended after she'd left a bar with another man.

"If you've got enough character to let the relationship progress without compromising your faith, then. . ." Jesse shrugged. "I don't see a problem with taking prayerful steps forward. But I do think Trevor's right: You have to be honest with her about your faith."

"I agree with that part, but I don't think you should move ahead in this relationship one more inch." Trevor shook his head. "You're playing with fire. Unbelieving women in this day and age have no scruples, no shame."

"That's quite the generalization there, Trev." Luke reclined at the end of the couch. "I think there are a lot of non-Christian women with high moral standards."

"Well, maybe." A wave of chagrin washed over his features. "But my point is that this sort of thing is exactly how good Christian men end up falling into sin."

"Anyone can fall into sin at any time," Jesse argued the point. "When a believer isn't walking in the Spirit, he's walking in the flesh and that's when he's in the danger zone."

Luke remained silent, weighing both sides of the debate.

"Dude, there's got to be half a dozen godly single women at church who'd welcome your attention." Trevor gazed at him with a mix of confusion and conviction in his expression. "Why don't you pray about God's leading with one of those women?"

"That would make sense, wouldn't it?" Luke had asked himself that question at least one hundred times over the last few weeks.

Seconds later, all conversation ceased as two of his three boys burst in through the front door. Except for the ice cream stains on their shirts, they looked none the worse for wear, and they each wore a sunny smile.

"We're home, Daddy!" Aaron came to a halt at Luke's knees.

"I see that." He pulled his son into his arms and gently roughhoused with him. They hadn't had any kind of makeup time since Aaron's discipline this afternoon.

The boy giggled when Luke tickled him.

"Did you have fun?"

"Yes." Aaron laughed so hard his knees buckled and he landed in a heap across Luke's feet.

Luke decided to target Devin now, since he stood by, grinning.

"Were you good mannered?" Luke grabbed him and tickled him.

"Ye–he–he–es," he tried to reply while laughing.

"That's my boy." Luke kissed his cheek and followed up with a playful swat on the backside.

"Let's do tickle torture." Devin's expression said he was all about that game.

Aaron popped up off the floor. "Yeah!"

"No. We have company and—" Luke glanced around. "Where's Miss Ciara?"

"She's coming." Aaron attempted to instigate the mass tickle session, but Luke caught his little arms and crisscrossed them around his chest, locking him in place with his knees.

"Now I got you, you little monkey."

Jesse lazed back on the sofa. "Man, I'm feeling right at home."

Trevor chuckled.

Finally Ciara strolled in, holding Brian's hand. Luke realized the little guy had been crying.

Luke whispered a word of warning to Aaron before setting him free. Then he stood. "Problems?" He looked from Brian to Ciara.

But before she could answer, Brian filled him in. "I fell down, Daddy." He pulled up the hem of his shorts and pointed at his knee.

His brothers stooped to get a closer look at the scrape.

Aaron appeared concerned when he turned to Luke. "It's bleeding!"

"I couldn't grab him in time; he tripped on the curb." Ciara wore a pained expression.

"Don't worry about it. Kids fall all the time." He looked at Devin. "Want to get the plastic bandages for me? And bring the green spray, too." Glancing at all the adults, he interpreted as Devin took off to do Luke's bidding. "The boys call the antiseptic the 'green spray.'"

Brian pouted, and Ciara swung him up into her arms. Luke hid a smirk, thinking his son was playing the sympathy card, big time.

"It's okay, honey, you'll be all right." Her voice sounded soft, soothing—motherly.

"It's a skinned knee." Jesse grinned. "He'll survive. Trust me. Mandy and I are at the Urgent Care Center a couple times a week, it seems, with our brood. Oh, and by the way. . ." He stood and extended his right hand to Ciara. "I'm Jesse Satlock. I believe I met you at Jen's when she had that jewelry party last year. I dropped my wife off and poked my head in the door to say hello but didn't stay."

"Yes, I thought you looked somewhat familiar." Ciara gave him a polite smile and freed one hand, shaking his politely. "Nice to see you again."

"I'm Trevor Morris." He, too, took Ciara's hand, gave it a friendly shake, adding a nod of greeting.

"Good to meet you."

She glanced at Luke, but before he could react, Devin returned with the bandages and antiseptic spray. Luke cleaned up Brian's knee while Ciara held him.

"What a production, Luke. Good grief."

"Oh, don't be such an insensitive lout." The bit of sarcasm earned him good-natured snickers from his friends. Ciara, on the other hand, didn't look amused. Luke was quick to apologize. "Inside joke. Came from a men's retreat we all attended years ago. Don't mind our strange sense of humor."

"Mmm."

She arched a brow in mild reprimand, and Luke thought she reacted much the way both Mandy Satlock and Grace Morris would if they were here with their husbands.

Jesse must have noticed the same thing. "Say, Ciara, what are you doing on the Fourth? Mandy and I are having a few friends over for a barbecue. You ought to come. It'll be fun, but we don't have to invite Luke and his bad jokes, but, um. . ." He glanced at the three boys. "You guys are welcome."

"Yeah! Party! Party!" Aaron pumped his arms up and down, and even Brian came to life.

Trevor snorted a laugh.

"Where does he get this stuff?" Luke couldn't imagine. "He's five years old!" He quelled Aaron's reveling by placing a hand on the boy's shoulder.

"So what do you think, Ciara?" Jesse leaned forward. "Think you'll come to the barbecue—even if Luke does show up?"

She set Brian on the carpeted floor. "Thanks, but no. I have to finish my master's thesis. That's the whole reason I'm renting Jen's condo next door. For some solitude. I got an extension today, but I still might not make the deadline."

"Master's thesis, huh?" Trevor seemed impressed.

"Ciara is writing about how 'ineffectual' fathers are, and she's using me as a prime example."

"Nice." Jesse hung his head back and hooted. "Are you serious?" He looked from Luke to Ciara and back to Luke again.

"Easy, now, I'm doing my best to prove her wrong."

Ciara shifted, looking a tad uncomfortable. "Luke, you make my theory sound so petty. I'm really presenting the case on an extremely high intellectual level."

"So you're saying we're too dumb to understand it?" Trevor smirked.

Devin pulled out his blue plastic case filled with small cars, and the boys began playing with them on the coffee table.

"On the contrary; I have no idea what your intelligence level is, so why would I comment on it?" She eyed Trevor in a way that made him back off.

Luke felt like things were turning ugly fast. "Look, this is all my fault." He glanced at Trevor, then Jesse. "I like to tease Ciara about her viewpoints, and she dishes it right back at me." He turned to her. "I wasn't insulting you or trying to get my buddies here to gang up on you over your thesis."

"No harm done. In fact, I enjoy batting ideas around."

"I like batting, too," Devin said, popping into the conversation. "And pitching. I got my own mitt."

Luke smiled at his eldest son's interpretation of the topic and tousled his hair.

Aaron and Brian shouted out their love of baseball, too.

"The Weldons are a competitive bunch," Jesse commented with a grin.

"That we are." Luke turned to Ciara again. "And I'm still determined to prove your theory wrong."

She softened, right before his eyes. "Well, you've succeeded... sort of."

He raised his brows, amazed at the partial admission.

A hint of a grin curved her pretty pink mouth. "It's true that I am using you as an example of a single father, struggling through day-to-day issues, but I've decided on more of an objective slant. Not all fathers are 'ineffectual.'"

"Oh, yeah?" Luke felt rather pleased.

"Pat yourself on the back, Luke. You're a good dad."

Luke was touched by the compliment. Meant a lot coming from her. What's more, both Trevor and Jesse appeared impressed by Ciara's kind admission. "Thanks."

But a second later, Aaron decided to slug Devin, who gave his younger brother a return shove.

"Da—ad!"

"Knock it off, you two." Luke decided the good Lord sure knew how to keep him humble.

Trevor and Jesse both donned empathetic grins.

"I want you three to go upstairs, wash up, brush your teeth, and change into your pajamas. *Now.*"

The boys did as he asked but stomped their hardest and loudest as they made their way to their bedroom.

Trevor stood. "I'd best be leaving. I need to help Grace get our kids to bed."

"Me, too." Jesse's remark came out like a weary sigh. He pushed to his feet and tossed a challenging glance at Trevor. "Bet it takes Mandy and me three times as long to get our six children tucked in for the night as it takes you and Grace."

"I'm sure it does." Trevor grinned.

Luke didn't add that it sometimes took him half the night to settle his rambunctious boys.

"Six kids?" Ciara seemed to have parked on that particular piece of Jesse's remark.

"Yes, indeed." A proud smile curved his full lips. "Four girls and two boys."

She turned to Trevor. "And how many children do you and your wife have?"

"Just two. But they're blessings enough for Grace and me." He ran a hand over his balding head. "They're both ten going on twenty-one, and I'm lucky I have any hair left at all." He chuckled.

Luke grinned and saw his buddies out the door. He noticed Ciara hung back, and he felt both delighted and dismayed.

He closed the front door after thanking both Trevor and Jesse for stopping by and then turned to face the reason he'd asked his friends over in the first place.

nine

"Want some help putting the boys to bed?"

Luke shook his head. "No, I can manage. Thanks anyway."

Still attired in the striped tank top and jeans from this morning, Ciara took a step toward him. A small frown pleated her brows. "I'm beginning to think I've offended you. Have I?"

Again, he shook his head. "What gave you that idea?"

"You did." Her attempt at a smile wavered. "This afternoon you were brusque with me, but I attributed it to your being stressed from taking care of sick kids. Who wouldn't be? But now I get the feeling it's more than that. I mean, I sense some remoteness on your part."

She was a perceptive woman. No doubt about it.

Luke set his hands on his hips and glanced up the stairs, thinking it sounded like the boys weren't getting into trouble—yet. When he looked back at Ciara, he wondered how he could explain why their different beliefs made it impossible for him to get too close to her.

"Did my feministic viewpoints offend you? I realize I can come on strong that way, but I really do like you, Luke, and as much as I hate to admit it, you're living proof that a father is very beneficial to a family unit."

"Beneficial? Try *necessary*."

Ciara brought her chin back at his curt reply. "In your case, definitely necessary."

Luke swallowed the desire to share his beliefs. He hadn't intended to argue with her. "Listen, I didn't mean to bark at you. But I wish you'd see that a father is a key figure and role model for his children, Ciara. That's the way God designed families, with a mother *and a father*." He stressed the last three words.

"You're talking about old-fashioned ideals, Luke. But families come in all shapes and sizes: single parents, step-parents and blended families, foster families—you get the idea. But I can tell you that, from my research and experience, your parenting skills, as a single dad, are an anomaly."

"I appreciate the compliment, but—"

"Most single dads are like Chase Tibbits."

"Chase? What's he got to do with anything?"

She slipped her hands into the front pockets of her jeans. Luke thought he saw a hint of guilt in her expression. "The boys will probably tell you that we saw him and Jeremy at the ice cream parlor."

"Oh?"

"Chase insisted on sitting at the same picnic table outside with us, even after I warned him that your kids were recovering from the chicken pox. He wasn't concerned about his son catching it. But I was leery of him after the incident a couple of weeks ago. Seeing as your kids were with me, I didn't protest." Ciara pursed her lips, and she looked livid. "Almost immediately, Chase started belittling Jeremy and it made me so mad. The kid's only about a year older than Devin." Pulling her hands from her pockets, she raised them, fingers splayed in frustration. "I sat there fuming and feeling so sorry for that child while Chase picked at him for everything from not wiping ice cream off his mouth to not catching the baseball at the park. When it was time to go, I pulled Chase aside and gave him a piece of my mind." Remorse crept over her delicate features. "But I didn't realize that your kids overheard. They were supposed to be climbing into the van."

Luke rubbed the backs of his fingers alongside his jaw. "Were you using bad language or something? I'm not quite sure I understand the whole problem."

She shifted. "I called Chase a jerk, but that's as bad as I got. Chase, on the other hand, used some, um, colorful verbiage with me until I reminded him that I didn't call the cops after

I caught him prowling inside Jen's condo. That finally shut him up."

"Mmm. . ." Luke thought it over. "Well, my sons know using colorful verbiage calls for disciplinary measures."

"Luke, I feel just awful about them overhearing my disagreement with Chase. But I felt that I had to stick up for Jeremy." Ciara strode toward him. "My heart kept breaking and my ire kept mounting every time the man opened his mouth and picked on his son." She wagged her head remorsefully. "You trusted me when you allowed me to take your kids out tonight, Luke, and I guess I feel I let you down."

"You didn't."

"Okay, good." She tipped her head back. "So what's with the weird distance I'm sensing from you lately? I wouldn't have taken it personally, except that you seemed more like yourself when your friends were here. Once they left, I felt like a wall went up or something."

"It's difficult to explain."

She looked like she'd just taken a blow on the chin. "So I'm not imagining it."

"No, you're not imagining it." In spite of his gentle tone, a wounded expression clouded her face. "Please don't feel hurt. But just like you have your principles, I have to stay true to my beliefs, my faith."

"That's fair." Her words belied the bewilderment in her eyes.

But before Luke could explain further, a plaster-crumbling crash sounded from above. He tensed. Aaron was parachuting again.

"Scuse me, Ciara. We'll have to finish this discussion later."

"Sure."

Luke took off for the steps.

❧

Cici returned to Jen's condo, trying to shake off her feelings of rejection. She and Luke were opposite in every way; how had she ever developed feelings for him?

Maybe they weren't real feelings at all. Perhaps it had been mere attraction and nothing more from the start. Cici had studied cases in which women entered into all sorts of commitments based on fluttery feelings that soon faded like denim.

Women such as Bridget and Tanya. Cici began to fume. How dare they accuse her of being "in love"! What a laugh. What did they know about love anyhow?

Cici showered and, afterward, pulled on a pair of loose-fitting, silky-soft turquoise capris and a matching sleeveless tank. She felt refreshed and less remorseful. After all, there was no reason that she and Luke couldn't at least be friends.

Picking up her computer, she ambled downstairs and into the living room where she booted up the laptop and then turned on the television for a little background noise. She retrieved a cold bottle of flavored water from the fridge and then got comfy on the sofa.

She'd written only a few paragraphs when the doorbell rang.

Standing, she assumed it was Luke, since he'd said they'd finish their conversation later and no one else she knew would stop over at ten o'clock at night. So she was stunned to find Chase Tibbits standing on the front stoop.

"What are you doing here?" She noticed the grocery store bouquet in his hand.

"I came to apologize."

"Oh?" Cici didn't think he seemed intoxicated.

He held out the flowers. "You were right. I was a jerk tonight and I feel bad about the way I treated Jeremy. My dad did that same thing to me and I resented him most of my life."

She accepted the blooms, albeit with a good measure of hesitancy. "Where's Jeremy?"

"Sleeping. A neighbor's with him."

Cici was glad to hear the child wasn't alone, but she still didn't know what to make of Chase and his floral peace offering.

"I also want you to know that I'm sorry about coming in uninvited a couple of weeks ago. Guess I thought you'd like my company." His gaze roved over her in a way that made Cici feel like running upstairs and cocooning herself in Jen's thick terrycloth bathrobe.

In that moment he didn't seem like any less of a jerk than he had earlier this evening.

"I think you need to leave." She handed back the bouquet, but Chase wasn't quick enough, and the flowers landed at his feet.

"Hey, now hold on." With one meaty hand, he blocked her attempt to close the door. "I don't mean any harm, here. I came to apologize. . .for Jeremy's sake."

At the mention of his son's name, Cici refrained from slamming the door in his face. "What do you mean?"

"You're good with kids. That's obvious. I think you could be a positive influence in Jeremy's life. Maybe help me undo all the damage I've done."

"How would I do that?"

"I don't know." Chase lifted his brawny shoulders. "Maybe like the same way you're helping out Luke next door here. Me and him—well, we're sort of in the same boat, being single dads. It's tough, and I've got Jeremy for the next two weeks by myself."

Cici didn't feel an ounce of pity for him, but her heart bled for Jeremy. "You need a babysitter, is that what you're telling me?"

"No, no, no." Chase shook his head. "I need a friend. That's all. Someone who likes kids and can steer me down the right path as a dad."

Might be an act, although Cici thought he appeared genuine. Maybe he was—this time.

She watched as he bent to scoop up the bouquet of flowers. He held them out to her again. "For starters, you could come by on the Fourth. I'm having a little cookout in the backyard. Nothing fancy. Burgers on the grill and a case of beer. But you don't have to come if you're busy." Chase ducked his head, looking like a little boy.

Cici couldn't find it within herself to be completely heartless. After all, everyone made mistakes and here Chase was, standing at the doorway, admitting his transgressions and apologizing for them.

For the second time, she accepted the flowers. "Thanks—and maybe I'll stop by."

A grin split his face. "Well, hey, then I'm glad I stopped by."

Cici gave him a parting smile before slowly closing the door.

&

Luke stood at his front screen door. He hadn't meant to eavesdrop, but when he'd heard Chase's booming voice through the open living room window, he thought it might mean trouble for Ciara. He hadn't heard the entire conversation; however, he'd gotten enough of an earful to realize that Chase was doing exactly what Luke had determined never to do: use children to bait a woman. By the sound of it, Ciara fell for the tactic—or had she just been polite in order to get Chase off her doorstep?

Setting his hands on his hips, Luke mulled over his discussion this evening with Ciara. He'd been surprised to discover she'd left while he'd tucked the boys into bed. He had presumed the two of them would continue talking once the kids were settled and he came back downstairs.

Lord, I didn't mean to hurt her. . .and now she's considering Chase Tibbits's invitation for the Fourth of July? After he acted like such a creep? So what if he apologized!

Luke had to admit it: He felt jealous. He didn't know what to make of his feelings, although he did know one thing for sure. He wasn't about to step aside while Ciara spent the upcoming holiday at Chase's place.

He climbed the steps and checked on his sons. Taking in their peaceful expressions, he smiled. They were sound asleep. Crossing the room, he switched on the monitoring system, which he habitually did when he planned to be either outside or in the basement for more than just a few minutes. In his office, he pocketed the small counterpart from which he would be able to hear if his kids awoke.

Then he headed over to Ciara's. God willing, she'd come back to his place where they could finish their earlier conversation, and maybe he could convince her to spend the Fourth with him at Jesse and Mandy's house.

❧

Cici had just reread the last paragraph she'd written on her thesis when the back doorbell sounded. This time she was sure it had to be Luke. Setting aside her laptop, she rose from the sofa and strode through the kitchen. She opened the back door and there he stood.

"Come on in."

He pulled open the screen door and stepped into the kitchen. Cici saw his gaze take in her pajama-like attire, but unlike Chase's lusty stare, Luke's held a light of appreciation, and it made her think maybe he harbored feelings for her after all.

"So what brings you over?" She folded her arms.

"Well, um, I was hoping we could finish talking." Luke rubbed his jaw in a way that Cici had come to know meant he felt uneasy or dismayed.

"Sure. I've got some time." She abandoned all hopes of writing more tonight but determined to start in on her thesis bright and early in the morning. "Why don't we sit down in the living room?"

"I had hoped you'd come over to my place. I don't like to leave the kids for too long, even when they're sleeping. I know from experience that once you and I get talking it's easy to lose track of time."

"True." Cici couldn't completely restrain her smile. The fact they'd been able to converse on a comfortable level had to mean they were friends.

He stared at something on the counter, and Cici followed his gaze to where the plastic-wrapped flowers lay. She'd forgotten all about putting them into water.

She turned back to Luke. "You'll never guess who those are from."

"Chase Tibbits."

A sense of surprise filled her being.

Luke must have seen it on her expression. "I overheard some of your conversation with him tonight. I honestly didn't mean to eavesdrop, but when I heard his voice I got concerned, especially after what you said happened at the ice cream parlor."

Cici was touched that Luke cared. "Nice of you to look out for me, but you honestly don't have to bother. You've got enough in your own home to manage. Besides, I'm a big girl. I can take care of myself."

"I know you're a capable woman, and I never meant to imply otherwise. It's just that I think Chase was feeding you a line, and I hope you're not swallowing it."

"Of course I'm not." She suddenly felt stupid for even briefly believing Chase was sincere. "I'm just concerned for Jeremy."

Luke took a step toward her. "You've got a heart for kids and Chase can see it. Maybe part of what he said is true—he'd like some help raising his boy. Every parent needs guidance and assistance from time to time. But I'm of the opinion that Chase has dubious intentions."

Cici tipped her head and regarded him. If she didn't know better, she'd think he was jealous. But that was absurd—wasn't it?

"I never meant to hurt your feelings, either." Luke's voice sounded soft, gentle. "I can tell I did, but if you could give me a chance to explain further—"

"Oh, it's no use, battling theories. Let's just agree to disagree and be friends."

"Ciara. . ." He glanced at the ceiling and chuckled incredulously. "That'll never work for me." He looked back at her and then stepped forward and placed his hands on her upper arms. She felt the warmth of his palms on her skin. His mouth moved as though he struggled with the words he wanted to say next. But the glint in his eyes said it all.

She knew in that instant that Luke's feelings mirrored her own.

Cici's arms intuitively encircled his waist. She stood on tiptoes, touching her lips to his. It took a second for him to respond, but when he did, Cici was unprepared for the rush of emotions that flooded her. The whole world suddenly went away. All that mattered was this very moment in which she and Luke fit each other like the final brush strokes that completed some beautiful yet dramatic work of art.

"No more, Ciara." In one abrupt move, he pushed her away.

"What's wrong?"

He let out a sigh and his breath touched her cheek like a feather.

"I've never been kissed like that." She couldn't seem to help blurting out the remark, although it earned her a little grin from Luke. "It felt so right; why did we stop?"

"Because things that shouldn't be happening are—and they're happening too fast between us. What just occurred only proves it."

"Too fast?" She stared up into his face, trying to understand.

"I've been fighting my feelings for you since we met."

"So that's it—the reason for your intermittent standoffishness?"

He turned, leaned against the counter, and folded his arms. "I'm sorry, Ciara."

"Why are you sorry?" She stepped in front of him. "And why are you battling your emotions?"

"Because. . ." He swallowed hard as he touched one of her curly tendrils, still damp from her shower. "When I fall in love again, I want to be sure I'm following God's plan as well as my feelings, but God's plan has to come first."

"Because you were hurt before?" Cici recalled what he'd told her about his wife, Alissa, how she'd likely been cheating on him. She nodded. "I certainly understand, Luke. I've been hurt, too, back when my dad walked out on Mom and me. The summer before I entered college I actually saw a therapist who helped me learn to overcome my issues of abandonment—and I'm still learning."

Luke opened his mouth to say something but swallowed the words instead. He dropped his arm to his side and looked across the kitchen. It seemed he was fighting more than just his emotions. She sensed there was more he longed to say but didn't know how to express it.

"Do you not want to see me anymore? Is that what you're telling me? Should we put some distance between us?"

His gaze flew back to her. "No." He shook his head as if clearing the fog in it. "Oh, I don't know. . ."

"I realize our philosophies on life are sort of at odds, but. . ." The last of her sentence stuck in her throat as she recollected something Jen once said. Something about how happy she was to meet William and fall in love with a good Christian man.

A Christian.

She wasn't one.

"I know what the problem is. It's your religion, isn't it?"

"Well, it's more than religion. It's my relationship with Christ—and, yeah, that's it exactly."

"Why didn't you say so?"

"I—I didn't know how to explain it in a way you'd understand. I mean, I didn't want to make my beliefs sound cultish or offensive to you. Faith in Christ is the most awesome thing ever." Luke's entire countenance lit up. "Talk about moving mountains and parting seas—it's all that and more."

Cici didn't know what to say, how to respond.

"But, concerning you and me, I'm trying to act on biblical principle, and you never told me where you stand on Christianity. You said you've got your own religion and asked me not to preach to you because William had already."

Cici couldn't deny it. "Point well taken, Luke. You're right. We never did discuss the subject of God—and it's one that's obviously very important to you."

"It is."

She thought it over, speaking what came to mind. "Spirituality is a very positive force in Jen's life, and it's something I admire in you, too. William, on the other hand, is a little too dogmatic for my tastes, but otherwise he's a likable guy."

Luke's features softened. "Are you open to, um, *researching* what Jen, William, and I believe?" A hint of a grin tugged at the corners of his mouth.

"Maybe." Cici felt hesitant and yet she didn't know why. She'd studied various world religions in college. She was hardly mindless and gullible. She'd draw her own conclusions. "Make that a definite maybe."

Luke smiled. "I'll accept the definite part of that oxymoronic reply."

In spite of herself, Cici laughed. But she didn't argue.

"How about starting off your research by coming to the Satlocks' with the boys and me to celebrate Independence Day?"

Cici felt torn between being totally responsible and having some semblance of a life. "I planned to spend most of the day writing my thesis."

"We're not leaving until about two o'clock. Gives you all morning to work on your paper."

If certain superheroes aren't bouncing off the walls and parachuting off bunk beds.

"Think picnic, fireworks. C'mon, you don't want to sit inside at the computer the whole day."

She sure didn't. Truth be told, she'd much rather spend time with him—and the reality of that inner admission shocked her.

"Ciara?"

He was waiting for an answer. "Oh, all right. You convinced me." She smiled, thinking Bridget and Tanya would be so proud. "Sure, I'll come along. It sounds like fun."

Luke strode to the door and then turned, as if on second

thought, and asked, "As for you and me: How about a *definite maybe* on that, as well?"

"You got it." She didn't have to think twice.

ten

Cici highlighted a page and a half before pressing the DELETE key on her computer. Hours of work disappeared from the screen.

She sat back in the leather desk chair and blew out a frustrated breath. She'd been doing her best to concentrate on writing her thesis, but the memory of kissing Luke last night lingered in her mind and made it impossible to think about the inconsequentiality of the male race.

A mere kiss and suddenly she'd rather spend the Fourth of July with Luke than write her thesis. What would Aggie think if she discovered this turn of events? Her professor would be aghast, appalled, and utterly disappointed in Cici's decisions of late. However, she couldn't base her life choices on whether Aggie would approve of them. Cici knew she had her own life to live—and what passed through her when she kissed Luke was unlike anything she'd ever experienced before. Perhaps the culmination of emotions she felt were some sort of sign that he was the one, and yet Cici's practical side said they were miles apart on some very fundamental issues.

Like religion.

Checking her e-mail, Cici hoped she'd hear from Jen. She'd sent off a list of questions about Christianity. In previous messages she'd mentioned Luke and finally admitted things were heating up between the two of them. But in this morning's e-mail, Cici made it clear she wasn't about to convert just because of her growing feelings for Luke; however, she felt strongly that she owed it to the both of them to at least investigate what he believed in and why.

But Jen hadn't responded yet.

Pushing the chair away from the desk, Cici stood and stretched. Then she wandered around her friend's office and paused in front of the bookcase. The volumes were neatly aligned and Cici scanned the titles. Her gaze stopped at a collection of C. S. Lewis's writings. She was, of course, familiar with the author and had read bits and pieces of his work, although she'd never been a fan of his *The Chronicles of Narnia.*

She grinned, thinking Luke probably enjoyed the series.

Cici pulled a book from the shelf and flipped it open to a random page. There she read: "A man can no more diminish God's glory by refusing to worship Him than a lunatic can put out the sun by scribbling the word *darkness* on the walls of his cell."

She blinked and read the words again, admitting the quote took her aback. In essence, Lewis claimed that God's glory wasn't lessened by those who didn't believe in Him, unlike politicians, popular movie stars, or renowned college professors who needed a large base of support in order to shine.

Interesting.

Cici took the book downstairs and pulled a cold bottle of flavored water from the fridge. Next she sat down at the kitchen table and began to read more from the published compilation. Before she knew it, hours had passed. She was amazed at how much time had gotten away from her as she stared at the kitchen clock; however, it was actually the sound of children's laughter outside that caused her to pull her nose out of the book. She stood and walked to the door, peering through the multipaned glass window. Luke's little superheroes were playing on their wooden play structure along with Jeremy Tibbits. All four boys wore bathing trunks.

Cici's gaze jumped back to Jeremy. What was he doing in the backyard? Did Chase know his son's whereabouts?

She stepped outside and sat down on the cement stoop by the back door that led to the patio. She was met by hot, thick air and a smoldering lick of sunshine. Having been in the air-conditioned condo all day, she hadn't realized how oppressive the heat and humidity felt outdoors.

"Okay, who wants to get wet?" Luke appeared from behind the fence and strode across the yard with the garden hose in one hand and a colorful plastic object in the other.

The boys whooped and cheered in answer to his question.

Cici watched as Luke screwed on the yellow, red, blue, and green attachment to the end of the hose before placing it on the grass. He walked back to the house and turned on the water. In no time streams jetted out the sides and top of the attachment and the kids began running to and fro, squealing and laughing. The happy sound made Cici smile.

"Taking a break?" Luke had spotted her.

"Sort of." She hoped she didn't look as guilty as she felt. She hadn't gotten any further along in her writing today.

Luke disappeared and returned a minute later with two folding lawn chairs. He set them up in the shade of a mature maple tree. "Come sit in the shade, or before long you'll look like a lobster."

Cici couldn't refuse his offer, although it had little to do with the possibility of sunburn.

"How's the writing going?"

She expelled a weary sigh as she lowered herself into the lawn chair. "Not so great. I got sidetracked today and ended up reading C. S. Lewis for hours."

"Narnia?"

Cici noted his enthused expression and laughed. "One of your favorites, I presume?"

He nodded.

"I knew it." Her smile lingered. "Typical superhero material. But, alas, I was reading excerpts from some of Lewis's more serious work."

"What do you think of it?"

"It's food for thought. I mean, the author had quite the intellectual take on God and Christianity, and yet the principles he wrote about are quite simplistic."

"Nothing about Christianity is difficult." Luke's gaze bore into hers. "Maybe, in some ironic way, that's what makes it so hard for some people to accept."

"Are you insinuating that I'm in the category as 'some people'?" She was only half teasing.

"No, not at all." A light of sincerity shone in his dark eyes. "I'm just stating an observation." He raised a brow. "Are you trying to pick a fight?"

She could tell he was teasing. "Me? Pick a fight?"

Luke chuckled. "I'll bet you were captain of the debate team in college, eh?"

"No, and for your information, I wasn't even on the debate team."

"Their loss."

Cici turned and rapped him on the upper arm.

He continued to grin, his gaze fixed on the boys who laughed and ran through the spriggles and sprays of the water toy.

"How did Jeremy get over here?"

"I thought you'd never ask." Luke looked her way. "I woke up thinking about last night—about how you said Chase had publicly belittled Jeremy and then came over to your place to apologize. I know it's hard to be a single dad, and I figured I could give the guy the benefit of the doubt. So, to show my support, the boys and I walked up the block to his condo and asked if Jeremy could come over and play. Chase agreed and Jeremy's been having a great time. Good for my kids, too, since they don't fight so much with each other when Jeremy's around to impress."

"Good for you, Luke." Cici was impressed that he'd selected to take the high road. But she couldn't help feeling a little wounded that he woke up thinking about Chase and Jeremy and not her—them.

"Well, I do have to admit that my intentions were twofold."

"Oh?"

"Yep. I figured I bring the research to you and save you the headache of keeping company with Chase." Luke glanced at his wristwatch. "He'll be here to pick up Jeremy in an hour or so. Feel free to interview him."

Cici suppressed the urge to laugh out loud. "Why, Luke Weldon, you act as though you're jealous or something."

He rubbed the back of his neck and then squared his shoulders. "It might seem that way." His voice held a note of amusement. "But I'm just trying to help you out."

"Sure you are." Cici smiled and shook her head. She wasn't irked by the fact that he'd manipulated the situation. Quite the opposite; she felt touched by his concern. On the other hand, she needed to let him know a couple of things about herself. "Luke, just for the record, I'm an independent woman, and I don't need to be guarded like a little girl. What's more, I'm loyal to my friends and those I love."

"That's good to know." He stared at the kids. "The loyal part, anyway."

She sensed he made a reference to his deceased wife.

"Well, I appreciate your sharing those qualities about yourself, although I'm already aware of your independence, and I think I've sensed all along that you're trustworthy. But I didn't invite Jeremy over here because of my own insecurities."

"Didn't you?"

Luke had the good grace to consider the question.

"Chase Tibbits is not my type, Luke. I'm not sure I'd even consider him friend material."

"But you're a bleeding heart, Ciara, especially when it comes to kids."

"And you think that because you and I met by way of my research and my love for children that I'll be tempted to fall into Chase's arms for the same reason?" Cici shook her head. "Have a little more faith in me. I'm not naïve."

Luke didn't reply, but Cici could tell she'd hit a nerve. She hadn't meant to hurt him in any way and yet the truth needed to be said so it could be dealt with out in the open.

She watched his expression and knew by the way the muscle flexed in his jaw that he was deliberating over her remark. She often wondered why he hadn't remarried. She'd met several single women from his church when they'd dropped off meals during the time the boys were sick. They were attractive. What's more, they seemed intelligent and pleasant enough. Cici just assumed Luke never connected with those women on any particular level, and that much might hold true. Although now she wondered if there wasn't more to it. Perhaps his insecurity over the way in which he'd lost Alissa was the real motive for avoiding becoming romantically involved again—

Until now.

Cici reached over and set her hand on his. He captured it in his palm. "I've been hurt, too, Luke. Remember how I admitted to having a general distrust of men on the night of the Condo Club's get-together?"

A little grin tugged at his mouth. "I remember."

"You said you had a general distrust of women and blew my mind. I never expected we'd have a common thread."

He gave in to a smile and finally looked over at her. "I'm not so proud that I can't admit my faults. Maybe a small sense of insecurity prompted me to invite Jeremy over to play with my boys. But I have a soft spot for kids, too, and you can't be so independent that you refuse to allow anyone to look out for you. That's a man's role. Protector."

"A man's role?" Cici groaned and yanked her hand from his. "Them's fightin' words, Luke. I suppose you think a woman's role is to be barefoot and pregnant."

"Well, not *all* the time." A twinkle lit his dark eyes.

His quip took some of the wind out of her sails but did nothing to deflate her indignation. "I think I feel like writing more on my thesis now." She stood. "Thank you for getting me stirred up again. It's just what I needed."

She ignored his smirk and marched across the yard toward the back door. But then, as she reached the stoop, she felt a blast of freezing cold water hit her shoulders and back. She shrieked and spun around to see Luke wielding the water toy like a bazooka.

The kids gasped and giggled.

He sprayed her again and she looked down at her now drenched pink and white striped seersucker capris and raspberry tank top.

"Thought maybe you needed to *chill out*, Ciara."

She replied with an indignant *yipe*.

He laughed, took aim, and fired again. This time she dodged the water.

She kicked off her flip-flops. "You're in big trouble, mister." She glared at him, although she had to admit the cold water felt rather good.

"Now get *us* wet, Daddy!" Aaron hollered, gesturing at his brothers and Jeremy.

"You're already wet."

"Get us some more." The boy wiggled his backside, taunting his father.

Of course, Luke couldn't resist, and Cici felt a wave of relief that his attention had been diverted. But as he chased the kids around with the hose, a mischievous idea of her own took shape. "Hey, superheroes, let's *get your dad*."

Luke sent a shower her way, but her suggestion hadn't fallen on deaf ears.

"Yeah, let's get him!" Devin said as if hailing the troops. "Let's protect Miss Ciara from the water monster!"

"Ha! I rest my case." Luke glanced her way. "Devin just proved my point. The desire to protect damsels in distress is an instinctive thing with us guys."

Those were the last words he spoke before being tackled by four knights in dripping swim trunks.

Cici took hold of the hose and made sure Luke got a face full of water. She laughed, but then her eyes met his and she saw his determined glint. She suddenly knew it was nothing short of war between them.

Luke stood, shrugged off the kids, and charged her.

Thinking of nothing but escape, Cici dropped the hose and ran. All at once, Luke caught her around the waist, clasping a firm hand around her left wrist.

"Ah-ha, now you're my prisoner." His voice, close to her ear, sent shivers down her arms in spite of the summer heat.

"The water monster has Miss Ciara!" Brian rushed toward them. "We gotta save her."

"Do you see what I mean?" Luke held out his hand and forestalled his son's head-butt. All the while his arm remained locked around Cici.

"You trained them that way."

"No, I encouraged what God already built into them."

"Whatever." Cici decided she wasn't in any position to argue.

He sidestepped the other three rescuers and actually lifted Cici off the grass as he inched his way toward the hose. She twisted and squirmed, fighting the inevitable: She was about to get the soaking of her life.

She wiggled and squirmed, trying to break free. "Don't even think about it, Luke."

"Think?" He laughed. "It's plotted and planned."

She gave out a little scream as the tip of the water toy touched her nape, sending a chilling cascade down her back.

"Don't worry, I'll watch the hair."

She elbowed him and, from the way he exhaled, she knew the jab was on target, but he still didn't release her. Instead he took turns spraying her and the boys who were still determined to save the day.

Then suddenly the flow of water stopped. The children fell silent, their little faces masked with confusion. Luke loosened his hold on Cici and, seconds later, all eyes came to rest on Chase Tibbits. He stood by the lawn chairs, cinching the hose in one meaty hand.

"What in the devil is going on here?"

eleven

Cici turned her head toward Luke and spoke out of the side of her mouth so only he would hear. "Nice going, *Water Monster*."

He released her and she stumbled forward. She wiped the water from her eyes and ran a hand through her soaking wet hair. With a glance down at her drenched attire, she decided there was no way to look even remotely dignified, although she gave it her best shot.

"We're playing with the kids," Luke told Chase, who seemed to be waiting for an explanation. "Want to join us?"

"Maybe." He gaze roved over Cici in a way that made her cringe.

"If you'll excuse me, I really need to change into some dry clothes."

She hurried to the condo, ignoring Chase's tawdry remark and subsequent laughter. When she entered the kitchen, she couldn't help but turn the lock on her back door.

She stared at it, marveling at how little she trusted Chase and how comfortable she was around Luke. Imagine playing right along with the kids! Cici hadn't had so much fun since she was a little girl—before Dad took off. But if Aggie had seen her, she'd have been mortified. Intellects didn't frolic in the grass and get captured by water monsters. As for Luke, he made one very irresistible foe.

Cici smiled. She had to admit, however, that she hated the way he'd so easily overpowered her. She'd done her best to break out of his hold without success. She was hardly a weakling. Who would have guessed Luke possessed such strength?

Next she imagined fighting off Chase—not in a fun water

fight, but in real life. There was no way she'd win. Even so, she refused to agree that Luke was right and women, particularly her, needed a man to protect or look out for them. Cici wasn't some poor, defenseless creature.

She squared her shoulders and realized she'd made a puddle on Jen's tiled floor. Tiptoeing to the sink, she grabbed a dish towel and tossed it over the tiny pool of water. Next, she ran upstairs to the bathroom and stripped off her wet clothes. She dried herself off, wrapped the towel around her body, and headed to the bedroom where she pulled on loose-fitting white cotton shorts and an oversized yellow and white Hawaiian shirt. It was her favorite lounge-around-and-do-homework outfit, but her hope was that its frumpiness would repel Chase's attention—if she went back outside, that is. She really needed to work on her thesis instead.

Laughter wafted up from the backyard. Crossing the room, she peered out the window. The boys had resumed their play beneath the spray of the water toy. Several feet away, Luke and Chase were sitting in the lawn chairs, talking. Things seemed amicable enough.

Stepping back, Cici had to resist the temptation to go back outside. She'd left her flip-flops on the stoop. But that wasn't a good enough reason to put off writing her thesis—again. Besides, three's a crowd. Luke and Chase seemed to be having a friendly conversation. No sense in her butting in.

Her decision made, she brushed out her tangled wet hair. Minutes later, she ambled into Jen's office and sat down in front of the computer. She reread the last several pages of her thesis, and just as ideas began to flow and her fingertips touched the keyboard, the back doorbell rang.

Cici groaned out loud and wondered whether to answer it. But as she weighed her options, someone pressed on the bell again. Was it Luke? Chase? One of the kids? Cici decided she just had to go see.

Down the steps, into the kitchen, and a moment later, she pulled open the back door to find Luke standing there. Dried grass had matted on the shoulder of his navy blue T-shirt. Remnants of their water fight.

She swallowed a grin and opened the door. "Hi."

"Hi. I'm going to light up the fire pit in about an hour. It's got a grate on it, and I told the kids they could roast hot dogs. Want to join us?"

She regarded him with mock incredulity. "Do you mean to tell me you're feeding your children hot dogs two days in a row?"

"Hold on." He held up his palms. "Before you give me the Worst Father of the Year Award, you should know that I made the boys and myself a vegetable quiche for lunch."

"You made a quiche?" Cici folded her arms.

"Spinach and cheese." He feigned an air of sophistication. "Only one of my many specialties."

Skeptical, she narrowed her gaze.

"Okay, okay, if you must know my secret recipe, I use an all-purpose baking mix, eggs, milk, mix it together, pour it over a bag of chopped, fresh spinach, add a few handfuls of shredded cheddar cheese, and throw it in the oven. It's actually very simple but tastes great."

"You're hardly a contestant for the Worst Father of the Year Award." Cici gave him a look of admonishment. "I'm really quite impressed, Luke."

"Impressed enough to dine by firelight tonight?"

"Well. . ." She surveyed the backyard. No sign of Chase.

Luke seemed to discern her thoughts. "He left; took Jeremy home."

Relief engulfed her.

He chuckled. "Coast is clear. C'mon out."

Cici felt a sting of remorse. "I'd like to, Luke, but I really have to finish my thesis."

"But you've got to eat, right? Have a dog and some pop and then work on your thesis later."

Cici hesitated to decline a second time. She'd like nothing better than to roast hot dogs with Luke and his boys.

"Say yes." He grinned and took a backward step off the stoop. "The kids are changing their clothes and then they're going to wind down for a while. After that, I'll light the fire pit-slash-grill."

"Oh, all right. *Yes.*" Maybe she'd get an hour's worth of work done in the meantime.

His smile widened. "See you in a while."

"Okay." In truth, she was looking forward to it.

❧

Luke watched his kids search for earthworms, each with his own flashlight in hand. Dusk had turned to nightfall and, against his better judgment, he kept tossing kindling into the portable fire pit to keep it aglow. The boys should have been in bed thirty minutes ago, but he just didn't want this evening to end. He thought he could sit beside Ciara like this 'til dawn. No teasing. No baiting and bantering. Just some of the best camaraderie Luke had known in a long while.

He glanced over and admired the graceful, easy way she sat in the lawn chair, barefoot, one leg crossed over the other. She seemed both amused and enthralled by his sons' antics, and she proved she wasn't afraid of brown, slippery, squirming things. She only reacted when Brian accidentally dropped his precious find on her thigh, and even then it wasn't a full-fledged scream.

As if sensing his gaze, she looked at him. They stared at each other for a long moment and then Ciara reached over and caressed his stubbly jaw. He caught her hand, embarrassed that his appearance wasn't the best. He'd been on the go since waking up and couldn't even remember if he'd shaved this morning.

"You're a pretty terrific guy, Luke, with incredible kids."

"Thanks." The compliment went all the way to his heart.

She worked her fingers between his. They felt both capable and delicate. "I have a confession. As silly as our water fight was this afternoon, it was more fun than I've had in about a decade." Beneath the light of the moon, he saw her smile.

"I was in junior high when my dad left home and somehow my childhood went with him, so it was fun to *play* this afternoon."

"Well, you know what they say: Work hard, play hard."

"Whoever 'they' are." She laughed.

Luke grinned. "Seriously, I play far too often. I probably ought to be more focused on designing software. But my boys are only little once, and I've found that playing with them is a great way to supervise. I can also teach them social interaction skills." Just then, Aaron clobbered Devin. He winced, and his eldest son's cry of hurt and anger seemed to fill the night. "Interaction skills like: Don't whack your brother over the head when you want the garden trowel."

"What?"

"Scuse me." Luke jumped to his feet and dashed across the yard, but he couldn't reach Devin before he socked his younger brother in retaliation. Aaron responded with fists a-flying.

"All right, break it up."

"Dad, Aaron won't give me the shovel."

"I had it first."

"Is that true, Devin?" Luke was growing weary of the fighting between these two.

"Yeah, but it's my turn." Devin pleaded his case. "You said everyone gets a turn digging and it was my turn, so I tried to take the shovel and Aaron hit me."

"You know better than to just take something, Devin. You should have called me instead of trying to wrestle it away from Aaron."

"But, Dad, Aaron knew it was my turn and he kept singing, 'You can't have the shovel. You can't have the shovel.'"

Luke turned to the habitual instigator. "Aaron?"

The boy just shrugged as though he didn't care if he were punished. . .again.

Luke looked up at the star-speckled sky and asked the Lord for wisdom. Aaron had been a veritable challenge in the last weeks, more than usual. Luke had tired of disciplining the boy hour after hour.

"Okay, listen, you were both wrong for hitting each other. Must be that you're overtired and can't think straight. Time for bed."

Devin moaned and complained. Aaron threw down the trowel and stomped toward the back door.

"Daddy, do I have to go to bed?" Brian stepped to Luke's side. "I didn't do anything wrong."

"No, you didn't, and I really appreciate your good behavior." He hugged his little guy around the shoulders. "But it's bedtime for you, too. Tomorrow's the Fourth of July, and we've got a busy day planned."

"Hooray! The Fourth of July!" Brian skipped to the back door.

"Ciara?" Luke spun around on his heel. "I have to tend to my boys, but I'll be out later to make sure that fire went out."

"Want some help?"

"No, I can manage. Thanks anyway."

"Dad, it's not fair." Devin's complaining recaptured Luke's attention. "Aaron started it."

"Lots of things in life aren't fair, son. Inside. *Pronto.*"

❧

Cici watched Luke round up his sons. Once they were inside, she settled into the lawn chair and closed her eyes. Off in the distance, she heard the sound of fireworks—a sound that would likely continue for the next several days—but all she could think about was how nice it had felt to sit beside Luke, her hand in his.

She allowed herself to dream just a little before thoughts of her thesis crashed into her mind. How did she ever expect to earn her master's if she didn't go inside, exercise some willpower, and write? Except, the wind had shifted and now a warm, gentle breeze made for comfortable backyard sitting. The sounds of a nearby bottle rocket and the smell of grass combined with the faint scent of wood smoke from the fire pit made summer come alive all around her. Suddenly Cici hated the thought of missing it. Besides, Iowa winters came too quickly and lasted far too long. And Luke said he'd come back out after the kids were settled. The latter, Cici decided, was worth waiting for, in and of itself.

Choosing to spend time with a man over writing her master's thesis? Aggie would be horror-struck by her lack of self-discipline in the face of such a powerful distraction. Cici herself was continually amazed. So how had this happened? How had she allowed it to occur? She'd set out to prove that men were inept and unnecessary when it came to raising children. It took a woman's nurturing, guidance, dedication, and love to produce healthy, happy kids and ultimately, well-adjusted adults. To her chagrin, Luke had proved her wrong on several counts.

However, she still believed he wasn't an average, typical father.

Cici heard a screen door open. She looked toward Luke's condo, thinking he was coming back into the yard and was surprised to see Aaron skulk out onto the stoop. He wore lightweight pajamas and shot a glance in Cici's direction. When she didn't respond, he inched forward, onto the grass. Slowly, the boy made his way to where the garden trowel lay. He picked it up, and Cici knew without a doubt that Luke had no idea Aaron had gone AWOL.

"Does your daddy know you're out here?" she finally had to ask.

Aaron shrugged his shoulders as though the fact was of little importance to him. He stared at the trowel.

"Nice shovel. Bet you found lots of worms, huh?"

The boy didn't reply specifically to her question. Instead he came toward her. "This used to be my mommy's shovel."

Cici was somewhat taken aback. "Your mommy's?" She didn't think he'd remember such a thing. He'd been an infant when his mother died. "How do you know?"

"Cuz." He paused. "I saw a picture of my mommy planting

flowers and stuff, so this was hers." He held up the trowel.

"Oh. . ." Cici realized interesting dynamics were unfolding. Had Aaron fought for the garden shovel, believing it was his mother's? Perhaps he had a deep-down longing to own a piece of his mother's memory—or maybe he longed to have a mom like other children his age. "I'll bet your mom planted beautiful flowers."

"She did." Aaron was at the side of Cici's lawn chair in a flash. "And I saw pictures of my mommy and us when we got born."

"Those must be special pictures for you." Without giving it a second thought, Cici hoisted the little boy up into her lap, dirt-caked hand trowel and all.

"Aunt Moira showed me. She's got a big, big book of pictures of my mommy." Aaron sat back and dropped his head against Cici's shoulder. He inspected the shovel with both hands. "Did you know my mommy?"

"No, I never did."

"You didn't?"

"No." Cici grinned, wondering if children's worlds were so small that they figured all adults knew each other.

"She died in a car crash. Aunt Moira said so and Daddy told me."

"Your daddy told me that, too. It's one sad shame, that's for sure."

"But she's in heaven with God."

Was she? Didn't seem to Cici that Luke's wife behaved very Christian-like, especially on the night she died. Of course, she'd never in a million years voice her skepticism. Who was she to judge? And if it made a little boy happy to believe his mommy was in heaven, then so be it.

"Miss Ciara?"

"Yes?"

Aaron laid the back of his head against her shoulder again. "Will you tell me a story?"

She smiled. "Sure."

"Tell me about a boy named Aaron and his mommy who planted flowers."

"Hmm. . ." Cici felt pained that the little guy obviously missed the mother he never knew. She wrapped her arms around him and gave the story some thought. "Okay, once upon a time there was a little boy named Aaron. He was a superhero who loved to dig for worms."

"Yeah."

Cici's smile grew. "One day he was digging and. . ." She groped for some religious thread to weave into the tale. Then she remembered the picture, hanging above Jen's headboard—the one with the warring angels. "And an angel came out of the sky."

Aaron twisted around to look at her. "Like Michael, the archangel?"

"Um. . .is Michael a good guy?"

"Uh-huh."

"Okay, sure, then the angel was like him."

"Cool." Aaron resumed his comfy position, his head feeling like a bowling ball now as it collided with her clavicle.

She winced but continued with her story, making it up as she went along. "So the angel came and told Aaron, the superhero, that his mommy was in heaven and that he shouldn't be sad. The angel said lots of people would come into Aaron's life and make him happy, like friends and grandmas and grandpas and aunts—and a good daddy who loved him." Cici didn't want to leave Luke out of the picture.

"What else did the angel say?"

"That—that every time Aaron planted a flower, seeds of happiness would be planted in his heart. And just when Aaron would need them most, laughter and love would spring up, just like tulips appear after the winter goes away."

Aaron turned so his forehead rested by Cici's chin. He yawned and didn't say more. She took his silence to mean that he was satisfied with her impromptu fairy tale. With a grin, she placed a kiss on top of his head. Within moments, the muscles in his small body went slack and his breathing deepened.

He'd fallen asleep.

Just then the yard light went on and the back door opened. Luke stepped out of the house. He spotted Cici with Aaron in her arms and marched toward them.

"Please don't be angry, Luke," she said quietly. She held out her hand when he reached the lawn chair. "He's asleep now. I think he just needed a little TLC."

"I think he needs a good *s-p-a-n-k-i-n-g*."

"Oh, Luke. . ." Cici grinned, hearing the facetious note in his voice.

"Seriously, this kid gave me quite a scare when I realized he wasn't in his bed and I couldn't find him anywhere."

"My fault. I should have brought him inside, but he asked for a story so I told him one." Cici slipped the trowel out of Aaron's grip and handed it to Luke. "He told me the garden tool belonged to his mother. I think he misses her."

"He never knew Alissa. Not really."

Cici disagreed, at least in part. "He knew a mother's love for the first year or so of his young life and. . .well, maybe he knows it's missing."

The conversation roused Aaron. He sat up and Luke lifted his son into his arms.

"Tell Miss Ciara good night."

"Night." It was the groggiest of replies as the little boy put his arms around his daddy's neck. Then he lay his head on Luke's shoulder.

Luke inclined his head toward the cast-iron fireplace. "Did it finally die out?"

"The fire?" She nodded. "Uh-huh."

She stood and when she looked into Luke's face, she read anguish in his expression. Alissa's thoughtlessness had been, undoubtedly, painful to deal with, but to think his son had been wounded in the fallout was probably excruciating for Luke. She empathized and cared, so it seemed only natural to try to comfort him.

She stepped in closer and touched her lips to his.

Just as last night, a dizzying sense of destiny fell over her, as though she and Luke were meant to spend the rest of their lives together. The *whiz, pop, bang* of a nearby firecracker seemed like confirmation.

The kiss lasted mere seconds, but Cici could tell Luke's emotions mirrored her own. He just fought his back because of his beliefs.

His beliefs—how could they be together forever if something so basic stood between them?

"I need to get Aaron to bed." His voice sounded soft and somewhat remorseful.

"Of course."

With slow strides, they both crossed the yard.

Luke seemed to regain his bearings first. "Thanks for your help with Aaron. I'll see you tomorrow. We'll leave for the barbecue about two in the afternoon."

"I'll be ready."

They parted at the fence, although Cici wished Luke would ask her over.

But he didn't. Instead he called a "good night" before entering his condo.

twelve

Luke could tell something was bugging Ciara from the second she stepped out the door wearing a red and white tank top and white slacks that stopped just below the knee. Her brown red curly hair was twisted up off her neck in an attractive, sort of disheveled way, but a troubled frown dimpled her right brow.

"Everything okay?" Luke tossed a duffel bag containing extra clothes for the boys into the back of the van. Then he lifted the cooler packed with ice and cans of soda pop and slid it, too, into the cargo area. "You seem upset."

"Jen called this morning."

Luke froze, fearing the worst.

Ciara must have read his thoughts. "No, no, she and William and all the others are fine. They're enjoying the trip."

Luke felt his shoulders sag with relief.

"It's just that Jen suggested I read a term paper she wrote for a religion class. She uploaded it from her computer to mine. I printed it and read it, and well, I found it deeply disturbing."

"Disturbing?" Luke glanced at his boys, climbing on the play structure in the backyard, and decided they were preoccupied and safe for the time being. "In what way?"

"The title of the paper is: 'The Infallible Word of God.'"

Luke nodded. Nothing seemed amiss to him thus far. "And?"

"Well, after suggesting I read her work, Jen told me that I need to believe that truth about the Bible if I'm ever to be able to understand Christianity." Ciara hitched her purse strap higher onto her shoulder and then slipped her hands into the side pockets of her slacks. "Jen's paper was hard-hitting, although she presented both sides, one from a Christian's viewpoint and the other as an unbeliever who thought the Bible was merely a nice book filled with moral stories and inspirational sayings." A blush crept into her cheeks. "I think she was quoting me."

Luke chuckled.

"But here's where I have difficulty with Christianity: I can't believe that a person who doesn't believe in Jesus Christ will be separated from Him for eternity, but that's what the Bible teaches."

"Yes, but—" Luke paused and prayed for both wisdom and boldness. *Lord, let me explain things to Ciara in a way she'll understand.* "The Bible also teaches that God is a patient, loving, merciful God who doesn't want one single person to perish. His desire is that everyone comes to that unique and intimate place of repentance, belief, and salvation, just the way it's written in the Book of Romans."

"The Bible."

"Right."

"So what it says in there goes?"

"That's what I believe. Yes."

"There's no gray area? Just black and white? Heaven or hell?"

He nodded.

"That's mind control, Luke." Ciara placed her hands on her hips. "When someone or something dictates a belief system as the right and only way, it's cultish and tyrannical."

He had to chuckle because at one time he had thought the same thing. "Ciara, try to look at it in this way: Our city here in Iowa has laws against stealing and murdering. If you break the law, you're going to jail. No two ways about it. Is that tyranny? Of course not. Now this great country of ours has a constitution. Do we live under tyranny because we're governed by all these. . .rules? No. Constitutional law is in place so that Americans can live in freedom here in the

United States. It's the same with God's Word."

She blinked in reply.

Luke hid a grin as he shut the hatch of the van. He dusted off his palms on his jeans, and then brought his fingers to his mouth and whistled a signal to the boys that they were packed and ready to go.

He looked at Ciara. "Still want to come to the barbecue today?" He hoped she hadn't changed her mind but couldn't help teasing her just the same. "We're a scary bunch, us Christians." He arched a brow, feigning a menacing expression and accent. "We might take possession of your mind and spirit, and you will become one of us."

Ciara whopped him on the shoulder with her purse.

He laughed.

The boys reached the van, breathless from their dash across the yard, and Luke assisted them inside. While they buckled up, he turned back to Ciara. "I'm sorry for making light of something as serious as your eternal destiny. It's just that before I became a Christian, I had the exact same opinions about Christians being cultish and all the rest of it. That's why I laughed. I hope you'll forgive me."

"I'll do more than that." She strode toward him. "I'll spend the day with you and your Christian friends and torture you all with my incessant questions."

"Bring 'em on." Luke opened the front passenger door of the van, smiling as Ciara climbed in.

❧

The Fourth of July partygoers consisted of Jesse and Mandy Satlock and their kids; Mandy's mother was in attendance, too, as well as Trevor and Grace Morris and their two children. Trevor's brother, Shane, had tagged along. He was recently divorced and, to Cici's dismay, Trevor tried playing matchmaker several times throughout the day. But she wasn't interested in the guy, although he seemed nice enough. All she had to do was glance across the patio and see Luke to know he was the one who had captured her heart. And when his dark gaze melded to hers, she could tell he felt the same way.

Trevor must have taken note of the way they shared fond looks and little smiles, and he made a habit of distracting Luke, sitting between him and Cici, and interrupting any conversation that sprang up between them. He made it clear he didn't like Cici getting too friendly with Luke; perhaps he didn't approve of her because she wasn't *one of them*. Maybe the matchmaking was his way of testing her morals.

Thankfully, Grace Morris made up for her husband's behavior. She had a keen sense of humor and sarcastic wit that had Cici laughing hard on numerous occasions.

And then there were the children. Cici observed that the Satlocks' and Morrises' kids, like Luke's boys, were well behaved for the most part. She especially enjoyed watching the fathers interact with their sons as they played a hilarious game of baseball.

When nightfall came, everyone piled into their vehicles and drove into Des Moines to watch the fireworks. During the spectacular display, Cici's new buddy, Aaron, insisted on sitting beside her, later crawling into her lap.

By the time they'd returned to the Satlocks', repacked Luke's van, gathered his boys, and headed for home, it was well past midnight and the little superheroes fell asleep in their car seats almost before Luke reached the first major intersection.

"Have fun today?"

"Definitely." Cici regarded Luke's profile, illuminated by the intermittent glow of the streetlamps they passed. "Except for the fact that your friend Trevor took a disliking to me, I'd say today was one of my more memorable July Fourth holidays."

"Don't mind Trevor. I plan to talk to him. He was totally obnoxious today."

"I got the distinct feeling that he doesn't think I'm good enough for you, Luke. Although, apparently, I'm good enough for his brother."

Luke didn't reply, but Cici noticed the jovial atmosphere had vanished.

"Anything wrong?"

"No. I'm just miffed at Trevor." He seemed to shake it off soon enough. "But aside from his embarrassing attempt to control the situation between you and me, you had fun?"

"Uh-huh. I had a great time. I really like Mandy. In fact, she invited me to a luncheon at your church next week and I said I'd attend."

"Seriously? You're going to the VBS Ladies' Luncheon? Our church's VBS—vacation Bible school—is next week."

"Yes, so I've been told, and, yes again, I am referring to that very ladies' luncheon."

"Awesome."

Cici settled back, thinking over her decision. "I figured, why not? Mandy said a dynamic local speaker has agreed to give a brief motivational talk, and the menu sounded delicious. I plan to ask my roommates, Bridget and Tanya, to come with me."

"Super."

Cici heard the enthused lilt in his voice and gave in to the urge to tease him. "But I don't want to hear any mind control wisecracks out of you."

"What about wisecracks about inconsequential dads?"

"They're off-limits, too." She folded her arms. It mildly galled her to wave the white flag of surrender, even at half-mast; however, Luke, Jesse, and even Trevor seemed polar opposites from the fathers she presented as examples in her thesis.

"I guess I have to admit that I may have been wrong in my generalizations and assumptions about fathers *and* Christianity, but I've done my research and I know inconsequential fathers abound in this world. There's also been brutality committed in the name of the Lord since the beginning of time."

"True and true."

Cici turned off the last of her defenses.

"On the flip side, there are responsible dads out there and

missionaries who proclaim the Good News who have suffered their fair share of brutality." Luke paused. "But I think God calls us to a balance, and it's a very delicate balance. A step one way leads to fanaticism and one step in the other direction leads to compromise."

"So what's the gauge?"

"The Bible, of course, and its promise that if Christians walk in the Spirit we won't fulfill the lust of the flesh, like the love of power, money, misdirected passions, and so on."

"Must be hard, walking such a tightrope."

"It's impossible, but that's where God's grace comes into play." There was a smile in Luke's voice. "He's the one who gives us the strength and wisdom to walk that tightrope."

"So when Christians fall, it's God's fault because He let them fall?"

"Sometimes it seems that way. As a dad, I watched in agony as my sons toddled around and fell while learning to walk, but I often took a hands-off approach. It wasn't that I didn't protect my sons; it's just that I know taking a knock or two is part of life—part of existing. Likewise, God, our Heavenly Father, knows He has to allow us a few bumps and bruises so we learn and grow."

"Makes sense." A second later, Cici realized the irony of her reply. She cupped the sides of her face. "I can't believe I just said that!"

To her chagrin, Luke laughed the rest of the way home.

thirteen

"Look, I'm sorry, man." Sunday morning, between services, Trevor shifted self-consciously in the crowded hallway of the church. He plunged his hands into the pockets of his brown trousers. "But I'm your friend, and friends look out for each other."

"I appreciate that, but you embarrassed me and you hurt Ciara's feelings and then, adding insult to injury, you tried to throw her together with your brother."

Trevor shrugged. "So? Neither is a believer."

"But we are, and, as Christians, we're supposed to be above all that sneaky, manipulative business."

Trevor conceded with a slight nod. "I apologize, although I think you're in too deep, Luke. You're getting too emotionally involved with this woman. Is she here at church today?" He glanced up and down the bustling hall. "No."

The comment didn't faze Luke in the least.

"You called me and Jesse over to your house less than a week ago because you felt like your resolve was slipping. Well, buddy, I think it's slipped. You should have seen yourself on the Fourth. You couldn't take your eyes off her, like you're under some kind of spell."

"That's ridiculous."

"And she couldn't take her eyes off of you, either."

"Yeah?" A surge of encouragement caused Luke to grin.

"It was embarrassing—and wipe that smile off your face. You're headed for trouble, dude. If you don't believe me, ask Jesse."

"I have already. Just this morning." Both Jesse and Mandy had a different take on the situation. Part of their more positive reasoning stemmed from the fact that Ciara agreed

114

to attend the VBS Ladies' Luncheon this week and she'd asked a lot of questions. Obviously, she was open to hearing biblical truth. But, as Mandy stated, there were critical days ahead for Ciara. She stood on the brink of a decision that would impact her eternity. The situation called for an enormous amount of prayer.

"Might be wise to put some distance between you and Ciara."

Luke shook his head. He wasn't about to turn tail and run now. "I can handle it. I'm capable of keeping my emotions in check."

"Couldn't keep your eyes in check on the Fourth of July, and if your eyes offend thee, pluck 'em out."

Luke recognized the words of Christ and would have taken them to heart, but Trevor had used them out of context. "For your information, my eyes did not offend me. I liked what I saw." Luke grinned. "Listen, all joking aside, I'm attracted to Ciara. I admit it. I like her a lot—maybe I even more than just like her. But I'm also aware that God has some miracles to do before I can pursue a serious relationship with her. She knows it, too. That fact alone has created a distance between Ciara and me."

Trevor didn't look convinced. "You deceive yourself, brother."

"I'll be all right. As long as I have a buddy like you who keeps me in his prayers and challenges me, I'll be just fine." Luke gave him a good-natured slap on the back. "I'm okay, you're okay. Okay?"

The jest wasn't totally lost on Trevor. "Yeah, okay."

❧

The sun began sinking into the western sky, and Cici sat on the front steps and watched its descent. The air hung thick and damp around her. Dark clouds moved in from the southwest, hastening the day's end, and off in the distance she heard the ominous rumble of thunder. Cici found the buildup to be rather exciting; she loved a good thunderstorm and Iowa certainly got its fair share. The only thing missing was Luke's arm around her shoulders, and she imagined how cherished she'd feel if he were here and together they watched the storm roll in.

Tossing a glance next door, she wished Luke would come outside. She hadn't seen him or the boys all day. She'd opted to spend most of the day at her favorite coffeehouse and work on her thesis. The usual bustling crowd was reduced to only a handful of customers because of the holiday weekend—and that worked in Cici's favor. Quiet for the most part, although she'd overheard snippets of intellectual conversations that reminded her of her determination and resolve to earn her master's.

That is until two middle-aged women, whom Cici recognized from the university, walked in. The pair sat at the table next to hers, and Cici couldn't help overhearing them. Within minutes, she found herself questioning everything she'd learned to believe, not because of what the women said, per se, but the way in which they said it.

The two talked only about hard-hitting topics as they shared the Sunday newspaper and sipped lattes. They praised a prominent female politician and insulted and denounced the men who made the news. Cici picked up on the bite in their voices and thought it seemed to rob them of their credibility. She hoped she'd never sounded so angry, so downright gauche, while expressing her views.

If she had, how had Luke put up with her this last month? Maybe she owed him an apology. Had she inadvertently insulted his gender while defending hers? A woman's worth had been taken for granted in this world long enough. She wanted to shout the equality message from mountaintops, but she hadn't meant it as a personal attack on Luke and she certainly didn't consider herself anti-male, of all things.

Suddenly Cici recalled how complete and utterly feminine she'd felt when Luke held her in his arms. Sitting forward on the front step, she allowed herself to revel in the memory and even fantasize just a little about how it might feel to be a bride, wearing an ivory satin and lace gown as Luke waited for her at the end of the long, white-carpeted aisle.

"Hey! Looks like we're gonna get some rain!"

The daydream vanished at the sound of Chase's booming voice. Before she could forestall him, he'd traipsed up the walkway and plunked down beside her.

She scooted over. "Mosquitoes are getting kind of bad. I'm thinking of going inside."

"Sure. We can do that." He pushed to his feet.

"Um, well. . .Chase, I'm afraid you misunderstood." She stood also. "That wasn't an invitation."

"Oh."

"I don't mean to be rude, but I'm just taking a little break from writing my thesis, and—"

"Right. Your paper. Well, don't forget my offer to be one of your research subjects."

"Thanks. I might take you up on it." She smiled and glanced around. "Where's Jeremy?"

Chase guffawed. "He's the reason I came over here—to pick him up and take him home. Jeremy's been playing with those Weldon kids all afternoon."

"How fun for him."

"And great for me. Tomorrow he's going to the Bible school with Luke's kids at their church. All week long I'll have my mornings to myself, which means. . ." He leaned forward in a conspiratorial way. "I can party and I don't have to worry about taking care of a kid while I'm hung over."

Cici was so appalled she couldn't think of a single intelligent reply.

"Then the following week my parents are coming to visit."

"So you have Jeremy for a two-week stint in all?"

"Yep." Chase swatted at a mosquito. "That's the trouble with divorces. Visitation eats up one weekend a month and sucks up two entire weeks during the summer—prime time for us contractors. But the ex and her lawyer got their way, so now I've got to pay for it."

Cici regained her bearings. "Why not try enjoying your time with your son? I wish my dad would have made time for me."

"Your folks divorced when you were a kid?"

She nodded.

"Too bad."

"It is what it is." She dismissed the matter, not wanting to discuss the particulars with Chase. She had a hunch he wouldn't understand anyway.

Just then four little boys burst out of the condo next door. They laughed and began running after each other in the front yard. Moments later, Luke appeared on the walk, wearing faded jeans and a light blue T-shirt.

"Thought I heard your voice out here, Chase." His gaze moved to Cici. He smiled. "Hi, Ciara."

"Hi, Luke." She stuffed her hands in her jeans pockets, feeling like a starry-eyed girl. She couldn't imagine what got into her whenever Luke made an appearance.

"Hey, since we're all here, why don't we hang out together tonight?" Chase looked delighted that he'd conjured up such a brilliant idea. "I'll bring over a six-pack, and maybe Cici here can impress us with her womanly skills by cooking up something for dinner."

"My *womanly skills*?" Cici turned to Chase and arched a brow.

Luke let out a long, slow whistle. "Buddy, you just said the *way* wrong thing."

"What?" He raised his shoulders in a helpless manner. "What'd I say?"

"Ciara's a feminist. You know, women's rights and all that." He sent a smirk her way. "Wouldn't be caught dead doing all that domestic stuff—like cooking."

"Not true." She pursed her lips in annoyance. "For your information, Luke, I can cook—and very well, I might add."

"I'll keep that in mind."

She grinned at the comeback and lowered her gaze. At any other time, she'd enjoy setting Chase straight about "womanly skills" extending beyond the home and into the workplace where women were equally as competent as men. Instead, recipes filled her head as she imagined preparing a delicious meal for Luke and his little superheroes.

Cici gave herself a mental shake and decided Aggie would be horrified by her rationale—or lack thereof.

"We can order a pizza." Chase's tone had lost some of its robustness.

"Actually, I'm bathing my boys and tucking them in early tonight." Luke set his hands on his hips. "Morning's going to come awfully fast. I have to pick up some other kids for VBS, as well as Jeremy, so I'll be ringing your doorbell before eight o'clock."

"Oh, right." Chase glanced at the boys darting around the front lawn. "I suppose I should get Jeremy to bed early, too."

Cici stifled a sigh of relief and considered asking Luke if he wanted some help with the kids. She soon thought better of it, suspecting Chase would impose on the offer. Besides, it'd be rude if she extended the offer to Luke in Chase's presence. "I need to get back to work on my thesis." She gave both men a parting glance and grin, but her gaze lingered on Luke several moments longer than necessary. She couldn't seem to help it. "Good night."

She entered the condo, feeling the sting of remorse. She would have enjoyed spending time with Luke and reading stories to the boys—and in all surprise and wonder, she realized that the whole homemaker role wasn't unappealing to her at all. She always imagined herself with children, but now she could see herself as a wife—Luke's wife.

She closed the front door and leaned against it. "What in the world is happening to me?"

❧

Lightning flashed and thunder cracked, shaking the very floor on which Luke and the boys had camped out for the night. When the storm approached, the boys had gotten scared and wouldn't settle down, even after Luke tried tucking them into his own bed. So he'd decided on a "cowboy campout," and arranged their sleeping bags in a circle. The kids took to the idea and, at long last, had fallen asleep.

Another blitz of lightning and the power went out. The television, on which Luke had been tracking the intense storm, flicked off. Thunder exploded as lightning illuminated the living room.

"Daddy!"

Luke set his arm on Brian's arm. "It's okay, son. I'm right next to you."

A second later, Brian was sleeping soundly again.

"Daddy?" This time it was Aaron.

"Yeah?"

"I'm wondering if Miss Ciara is okay."

Luke couldn't help but grin. Ciara had won Aaron's heart, too. "I'm sure she's fine," he whispered.

"What if she's scared?"

Luke pondered the question and guessed at her actions. "She knows we live next door. If she's scared, she'll come over and knock on the door."

"Yeah, and she can camp out with us."

Luke swallowed a laugh. That'd be real cute. However, he didn't bother explaining the impropriety of the suggestion because he knew Aaron made it in all innocence. "Aaron, it's really nice of you to think about Miss Ciara. I'm proud of you."

In reply, his little boy rolled over and set his head on Luke's shoulder.

"Now, go back to sleep."

"Okay, Daddy."

"Daddy?" Now Devin.

"Yes?"

"I think we should check on Miss Ciara."

"I'm sure she's just fine, but we could pray for her and let Jesus take care of her."

The guys liked that idea and settled back into their sleeping bags.

Eyes closed, Luke began in earnest. "Dear Lord, we come to You tonight asking for Your hand of protection over Miss Ciara and us. You calm the winds and the seas. This puny thunderstorm is nothing for You to take care of."

"Cuz Jesus is a Mighty Superhero!"

"Shhh. . ." Luke sensed Aaron was getting wound up. Amazingly enough, Brian didn't awaken. "We're talking to God now." Luke kept his voice low and calm.

Aaron quieted.

"Lord, You said 'peace be still' so we know we don't have to be afraid of storms or anything, for that matter." The situation with Ciara scampered across his mind. "You've got it covered, Lord. We love You and we thank You for taking care of us—and the people who matter most to us. We also thank You for keeping us safe. In Jesus' name. . ."

The boys ended the prayer along with him.

"Amen."

fourteen

"Hi, superheroes." Cici waved to the kids as she tossed out a bag of garbage late Monday afternoon. To her surprise, they came running over.

"Did you hear the big storm last night?" Devin's brown eyes were wide with curiosity.

"I heard a little thunder, but I fell asleep and slept as hard as a rock."

"Then our prayers worked!" A broad smile spread across Aaron's face.

"Your prayers?"

"We prayed God would make you not be ascared of the storm."

"That's sweet." She gave all three boys a little hug. "Well, I wasn't scared."

"I didn't pray," Brian admitted, accepting the hug anyway, "cuz I was sleeping hard as rocks, too."

Cici laughed and lowered herself onto the back step. She hadn't even turned on her laptop today but instead dusted, vacuumed, and cleaned Jen's condo. The epitome of procrastination.

"So how was your vacation Bible school this morning?"

"Fine."

"Good."

Brian stood by and bobbed his head in agreement with his brothers.

"Did Jeremy like it, too?"

Devin shook his head. "He got a stomachache, and I had to walk him to the office and they called his dad to pick him up."

"What a shame. I hope he feels better soon."

"His dad didn't come, though," Devin explained, "so our

dad took him home."

"Hmm. . ." Cici's opinion of Chase dropped another notch as she remembered how eager he'd seemed last evening to turn over the care of his son to Luke and the church's VBS program every morning this week.

"Our dad stays at church, cuz he runs all the computer stuff for the skit and for the pastor's talk."

Aaron and Brian affirmed Devin's statement with more nods, and Cici took in the proud expressions on all three boys' faces.

"Yo, guys! Where are you?" Luke's voice wafted over the wooden fence. There was an unmistakable urgency in his tone.

They turned to run along home and almost collided with him at the edge of the patio.

"We were talking to Miss Ciara." Aaron hung his head back to peer up at his father.

"So I see." Luke tousled his son's hair and smiled a greeting at her. "That's fine." He surveyed all three boys. "You've got another hour to play before supper and then it's showers and an early bedtime."

"But, Da–ad. . ."

Luke forestalled Devin's complaint with a stern look. Then all three raced through the yard to the play structure.

He watched them go, letting out a sigh that sounded both weary and relieved. "I always freak when it gets too quiet in the backyard."

"Can't imagine why." Cici laughed. She thought about how Aaron liked to parachute off the top bunk.

"Have we been too loud this afternoon?" He crossed the patio and sat down beside her. "I had Jesse and Mandy's two boys for a while, and the kids got kind of rowdy."

"Didn't hear a thing. Of course, I had the vacuum running off and on for the past couple of hours."

He turned toward her, feigning an expression of shock. "Cleaning? How domestic of you."

"Very funny."

Luke chuckled. "How's the thesis coming?"

"Don't ask." She set her elbows on her knees and rested her chin in her hands.

"That good, huh?"

Cici groaned. "I haven't even turned on my laptop today— not even to check e-mail."

"Writer's block?"

"I don't know. . ." Cici could hardly blame Luke for her inability to finish her thesis; however, it was he who'd crept into her thoughts throughout the day.

Silence hung between them.

"Are you still planning to attend the ladies' luncheon tomorrow?"

"Uh-huh." She nodded and turned toward him. "And Bridget and Tanya are coming with me. Should be fun."

A grin crept across his mouth and features so even his eyes seemed like they were smiling.

"Are you going to be home tomorrow afternoon? I'd love for you to meet my friends."

"Yeah, I should be around."

"Good." Cici felt pleased. She knew Bridget and Tanya would enjoy meeting Luke.

They talked for a little longer about friends in general, Luke's business, and again about Cici's thesis.

"Maybe you need a new direction."

"I've already strayed off the narrow path my professor laid down for me to follow."

"Well, here's hoping the guest speaker at tomorrow's luncheon gives you some ideas. I overheard some people talking about her today. Seems Beth Orana gives quite the motivational talk. A few guys were saying they planned to sneak in to hear her, although if Mandy's at the door they won't get by her." Luke chuckled as he glanced at his wristwatch. "Well, it's getting to be that time. I should feed my kids."

Cici stood just as he did. "What are you making for supper?"

"Not sure yet."

"Would you allow me to throw something together for you and the boys? We could eat dinner together."

"Are you trying to impress me with your culinary skills or procrastinate on writing your thesis?" He dipped his head so that his face was close to hers.

"Maybe a little of both."

Again, he laughed. "Okay, sure. If you want to make supper for us, I'm all for it. We eat just about anything."

"That makes it easy. Give me about an hour or so, all right?"

"Sure."

Smiling, Cici entered the condo and ran upstairs where she booted up her laptop computer. She logged on to a popular recipe site and found a famous chef's recipe for a "Cowboy Chicken Casserole" that didn't look too difficult to prepare. What's more, she was certain that Luke and the boys would love it—pepper jack and cheddar cheese, vegetables, and cut up boneless chicken breasts in a seasoned sauce all folded over tortilla chips and baked in the oven.

Perfect.

After printing the recipe, she hustled back downstairs and took a quick inventory. Then she listed the ingredients she still needed and hurried off to the grocery store.

❧

Luke prayed over their dinner and then dug in. His mouth had been watering for the last fifteen minutes, ever since Ciara arrived with the casserole. It smelled delicious and—

"Mmm. . .tastes great." He didn't think she'd mind that his mouth was full when he uttered the compliment.

His sons bobbed their heads but ate in silence. A sure sign they'd been starving.

"I'm glad you like it. I wasn't sure if it'd be too spicy."

Luke chewed and swallowed. "No, we like spicy stuff. The boys love salsa and chips during a good baseball game on TV."

"We like the Royals, but my grandma and grandpa cheer

for the Twins." Devin scrunched his face up.

Luke chuckled and interpreted for Ciara. "That's Kansas City Royals and Minnesota Twins."

"Got it." She took a tiny bite of casserole, chewed, and then swallowed. "Which set of grandparents live in Minnesota?"

"My folks."

"And the other grandparents are here in Iowa?"

Luke nodded. "They live in Des Moines."

Ciara seemed to digest the information, and he could practically guess the questions swirling around in that pretty head of hers.

"Alissa and I met at a Christian camp in Minnesota one summer. We were both camp counselors. Things progressed, we got engaged, and since she wanted to stay in Iowa, I found a job with a software firm here in Des Moines. We got married, rented an apartment in Des Moines, but eventually bought a house—in the subdivision where Jesse and Mandy live. But after the accident I sold the place and bought this one. I wanted something small and easy to maintain. Too hard chasing toddlers around a four-bedroom, three-bathroom home with a living room, dining room, and gigantic kitchen—which wasn't used an awful lot, I might add."

"My mommy was a good cooker, right, Daddy?"

He noticed the hopeful glimmer in Aaron's eyes and wondered about it. Maybe Ciara had been right about him missing his mom. "Right. A good cooker." Luke didn't add that she only heated formula and jars of baby food to perfection. Alissa's actual cooking hadn't been the best. They had often gone out to eat after they were married, and when Devin came along, she gave up preparing meals altogether. Luke had usually been the one to throw together a dinner when he arrived home from work, and they'd eat when the boys were asleep for the night.

When the twins were almost two years old, Luke began dining alone most nights while Alissa went out with her girlfriends. After her death, he wondered why he hadn't stopped her, hadn't insisted she stay home with him and their sons. But even his cajoling had sparked arguments, and Luke had wanted Alissa to be happy. So when she complained about being cooped up with the kids and insisted she deserved to go out with friends, he'd shut his mouth and tamped down his disappointment. It hurt that she hadn't valued his companionship. Still, he had trusted her. . . .

"And that's when you began your own business. Is that correct, Luke?"

"What?" Puzzled, he glanced at Ciara.

"After you moved into your condo?"

"Oh, right." He nodded, recalling that he'd told her how God had brought the self-employment opportunity his way. "Such a blessing."

As if sensing his troubling thoughts and disturbing memories, Ciara set her delicate hand on his forearm. Her touch somehow had a healing effect on him.

"I'm glad you enjoyed the casserole. Would you like a second helping?" She sent him a sweet smile. "There's plenty left."

Luke glanced at his empty plate and then grinned. "Don't mind if I do."

❧

While Luke washed dishes, Cici read to the boys and tucked them into bed, giving each a kiss on the forehead.

"You'd make a good mom." Devin sounded drowsy as he turned over in his bed, which was up against the wall adjacent to the twins' bunk beds.

"I'd like to be a mom someday." *I wouldn't mind being a certain software designer's bride, either.*

"We could use a mom around here to make cookies and stuff." Aaron yawned.

Cici laughed at the remark. Then she glanced at Brian who stared back at her with his soft, thoughtful brown eyes.

"Yep, you'd be a good mommy."

The comments earned each boy another good night kiss

on top of the head before Cici turned out the light and made her way back downstairs.

"You have the sweetest kids."

Luke was nearly finished loading the dishwasher. "Thanks."

"They went to sleep without a single complaint."

"They're exhausted."

Cici caught sight of the casserole dish, still coated with cheesy sauce and bits of chicken. She reached out and inched it toward the front of the stovetop. "I'll take this back to Jen's and soak it overnight."

"You sure?"

"Uh-huh." She smiled, noting Luke's expression of relief. "Positive."

An awkward moment passed.

"Dinner was terrific. Thanks."

"My pleasure." She ran her finger along the edge of the range. "Would you like to watch a movie together tonight?"

Luke hesitated.

"We don't have to." Cici ignored the swell of disappointment. "It was just a suggestion. I should work on my thesis anyway."

He caught her elbow as she lifted the casserole dish and turned to leave. "Wait, don't go. I'd like nothing better than if you stayed a while longer. It's just that—"

"I know; we agreed to take things slowly."

"No, you don't understand. It's not that. . ."

Cici set down the casserole dish and regarded him. "What is it then?"

Luke scratched his jaw. "Game's on TV."

"Game?"

"Royals. They play late tonight because they're in California." Luke headed for the living room. "Do you like baseball?"

"I never gave it much thought."

"Come on." He dropped himself onto the couch and patted the cushion beside him. "Have a seat." Next, remote in hand, he turned on the television.

Deciding that soaking Jen's casserole dish could wait until

she got home, Cici straggled in and sat down beside him. He slipped his arm around her shoulders as he pointed the remote at the screen.

"This is sort of an important game. Royals are having a bad year, but a win tonight could turn things around."

Cici cozied up to him and decided that maybe, just maybe, she could learn to love this sport.

fifteen

Cici left for home shortly after the game ended. In spite of having a limited knowledge of sports, she'd enjoyed watching the game with Luke. She could easily envision herself getting hooked on baseball and football—just so she could share that part of his life.

And what part of her life would Luke share? The debates over women's issues at the coffeehouse?

"Good night, Ciara." He'd kept an eye on her until she reached the back door of Jen's condo. Cici had insisted it wasn't necessary, but Luke, being the superhero he was, had been determined to see her home safe.

"G'night, Luke."

Glancing at the clear, starry sky, Cici realized there wasn't room for Luke in the academic cocoon she'd built around herself. In that instant, she also became aware of how alone she really was in the universe. Like the stars in the heavens, she'd become a solitaire among solitaires. Sure, she had friends, acquaintances, and colleagues; however, until now, she'd never known what it felt like to be inextricably intertwined in another person's life.

Upstairs, she booted up her computer, intending to work on her thesis, but thoughts of Luke wouldn't leave her mind. About a half hour later, she decided she was too fatigued to write, so she changed clothes, called it a day, and crawled into bed.

&

The next morning, the melodious tone on her cell phone woke her up.

"Ceece, you all ready for the luncheon? Bridget and I are leaving now to come and pick you up."

"What?" With the phone to her ear, Cici glanced at the clock, realizing she'd slept most of the morning away. "Oh, wow."

"Must be working really hard on your thesis, huh? You lost track of time?"

"I wish that were the case." Cici tossed off the bedcovers. "To be honest, I just woke up."

"You? Were you working into the wee hours of the morning?"

"No, I was watching a baseball game on TV with Luke and I was home before midnight." She sighed. "I haven't worked on my thesis in two whole days."

Silence.

"Tanya?"

"I'm in shock, okay?"

"Get over it and come pick me up." Cici laughed. "I'm hopping into the shower right now."

She ended the call and, although she said she'd "hop," she more or less dragged herself into the bathroom.

But thirty minutes later, she'd managed to come to life and had slipped into a pair of lightweight beige capris and a flattering rust-colored cotton blouse. She piled her thick, curly hair on top of her head, and she'd even gotten in a few sips of coffee before Bridget and Tanya rang the front doorbell.

The ladies stepped in while Cici slipped into her sandals and collected her purse.

"Okay, I'm ready."

They chattered like magpies on the way to the church and found their way to the multipurpose room in which the luncheon was being held. Mandy Satlock met them soon after the three entered through the doorway.

Cici made the introductions.

"I think I met you both a while back at Jen's jewelry party." An easy smile played across Mandy's full lips.

Recognition shone in both Bridget and Tanya's expressions.

"Follow me. I'd like you to meet some more of my friends." Mandy led them through the large, noisy room, stopping every so often to make introductions. Then, after about a half hour of the informal meet and greet, an announcement was made that lunch would be served.

Cici sat at the same round table with Mandy, Bridget, and Tanya. She was more than impressed by the smoked salmon and feta cheese wrap and tossed green salad. Simple, yet elegant.

When they'd finished eating, the keynote speaker took the floor. Cici guessed the woman was about forty-something. "I'm Beth Orana," she began, before listing her impressive résumé. "Did you know that godly women are meek? Are you meek?"

Cici sat back in her chair and almost groaned aloud. Bridget and Tanya glanced at each other, and then at her. Incredulous, Cici arched her brow but decided to give the woman a chance.

Beth grinned. "I suppose I should explain to you what most Bible experts interpret the word 'meek' to mean in conjunction with a woman's conduct. The world as we know it has perverted the word. I'm sure every woman in this audience cringed to think of herself as some sort of weakling or doormat. But that's not what I mean by meek."

Cici folded her arms, listening.

"Meek, in essence, means to possess a controlled strength. Like Deborah, a judge. Her story is written in the Bible; when a soldier asked her to come with him and lead the way into battle, she accepted the challenge. I mean, picture it: Charlton Heston as Ben-Hur, driving his chariot into battle, but only after *asking a woman* to lead the charge. Can you imagine?"

Many in the audience laughed at the visual and even Cici had to smile. She'd seen the movie on television, after all, and who hadn't read the classic novel?

"Well, the situation was similar when a soldier named Barak approached Deborah and said he'd go into battle but only if she went along with him. Barak stated that if she didn't go, he wouldn't either.

"Deborah agreed to it, lending him the courage he needed. But she wasn't a shrew or loud and overbearing. Deborah had a decided meekness about her, yet she was authoritative and possessed great leadership skills. But the victory wasn't Barak's. Or even Deborah's. It really belonged to a woman named Jael. She was the one who actually defeated the enemy."

Cici felt a bit amazed. The Bible recounted stories of women who were stronger and braver than men? Did that mean today's Christian women didn't have to swallow their ambition in order to please God?

She glanced around the room and noted the variety in the types of women in the audience. She was surprised to discover that she felt quite comfortable in their midst.

Beth continued talking about Deborah as well as other women in the Bible, noting their strength and courage was made possible only by God's grace.

Then she segued into the salvation message. "God's grace is available to anyone who asks. The apostle Paul wrote in his letter to the Ephesians that it's by grace we're saved through faith. What's faith? It's an exercise of your own free will. It's believing that what God says in His Word is true. It's with the heart that one believes and with the mouth that one confesses to salvation. The Bible says in Romans chapter ten that 'everyone who calls on the name of the Lord will be saved.'"

Cici had heard the Romans verse plenty of times before from Jen and William—and Luke, too. But somehow the passage never connected with her—until now.

Then suddenly everything she'd heard came to light.

"Ladies, forgive me if I sound preachy," Beth said, "but I must share the Good News with you. We hear so much bad news these days. That's why it's good to know, or be reminded, that Jesus Christ died for *you*—because He didn't want to spend an eternity without *you*. He loves *you* so much that He willingly went to the Cross when in fact He's God and could have summoned a host of angels to destroy His accusers."

Tears filled Beth's eyes, and Cici realized they were tears of awe and joy—like the tears brimming in her own eyes. "The very One who breathed the universe into existence deemed you important enough to come to earth and rescue you from an eternity of darkness and misery. Now, that is good news, isn't it?"

Light laughter flittered around the room.

By the time Beth finished her oration, Cici knew what she heard was Truth. She needed no more convincing; she'd seen Christianity played out in the lives of three very special individuals.

God, I believe. You're the real. . .Superhero.

Beth's gaze roamed the room and she smiled. "If you'd like to accept the free gift of salvation that God extends to everyone, it's very easy. You just take it—and tell Him. You can do so now, by praying along with me." Beth bowed her head and Cici did the same.

"Jesus, I admit that I'm a sinner who deserves the worst of punishments, but I believe that You died and rose again to save me. Please forgive my sins and come into my heart and live forever. In Your precious name I ask this. Amen."

When Cici looked up, another woman stood alongside Beth. She closed the session by inviting everyone to come back and visit again.

Applause broke out and everyone stood.

"So, what did you think?" Mandy stepped toward Cici so she'd be heard above the din.

"I think Beth's talk today was exactly what I needed to hear. . ." Cici paused before adding, "to believe."

"You?"

Cici nodded. "I asked Jesus to save me."

An expression of immense happiness spread across Mandy's features before she hugged Cici. "I'm rejoicing with the angels right now." She pulled back. "Come with me. I'd like you to meet a few more of the ladies here, and you really ought to say a personal hello to Beth."

Cici followed Mandy and spoke with several different women, including their speaker. After about forty-five minutes of chatting, she, Bridget, and Tanya made their exit.

"So what'd you think, Cici?" Tanya slid behind the wheel.

"Beth Orana's quite a good speaker and a nice person. She's sincere and I believed everything she had to say about Christianity." Cici pulled on her seat belt. "I've concluded it's the real deal."

"Seems like it." Bridget's voice drifted up from the backseat.

"I know it's the real deal. All I had to do was think about Jen during the luncheon and my decision was made." Tanya laughed. "I've never felt so encouraged in all my life. Christianity is exactly what I needed to start living again after the mess I went through with Ryan."

"Jen will be ecstatic. Two out of her three roomies got converted today." A smile tugged at Cici's mouth when she thought about telling her best friend. And Luke—she could hardly wait to inform him of her pivotal decision. He'd be ecstatic, also.

"Maybe a third roomie'll get converted, too." Tanya glanced in her rearview mirror.

"I'm still thinking it over," Bridget said from the backseat. "I'm not sure. . ."

Cici could relate.

"I attended religious schools growing up, and I'm not sure I want to go back to having all that religion in my life."

"Luke told me it's not religion so much as it's a relationship with God."

"Same difference as far as I'm concerned."

Cici pushed out a smile. "Well, you'll figure it out." It was one of those things a person had to struggle through on their own. Cici knew that now.

Tanya let Cici off at the curb. "Let's do lunch soon."

"Don't you want to come in for a while? Maybe Luke's home. I'd like to introduce you."

"Another time." Bridget suddenly appeared to be in a crabby mood. "I've got some things to do back at the apartment."

Cici didn't pursue the matter even though Tanya seemed

disappointed. She got out of the car and waved to her friends and then stood and watched the car drive away.

Once inside the condo, she heard sounds of laughter and peeked out the back window. She smiled at the sight of Luke sitting in the yard, his computer on his lap, while the kids splashed nearby in a wide, white plastic swimming pool.

She stepped out of the condo and he glanced her way. "Hi, Ciara. How'd the luncheon go?"

"Good." She trudged through the grass. "Excellent speaker. Marvelous meal." When she reached the shady part of the lawn where he sat, she held out her arms. "So, do I look any different?"

His gaze flicked over her and a little frown marred his brow. "Not sure what you mean. New hairdo or something?"

"No, you goof. I'm *one of you* now." She laughed, referencing his Fourth of July jest in which he equated believers to aliens from outer space.

He raised his eyebrows.

"It took me only minutes today to realize what Jen had been trying to tell me for the last couple of years." The smile lingered on her face. "Luke, I'm a Christian."

❧

Too easy. Couldn't be true. But as Luke and Ciara conversed for the next hour, he sensed something truly different about her.

She pulled up a lawn chair. "What's cool is I didn't have to change myself in order to be Christian. Somehow I assumed I had to dress and behave a certain way in order to be accepted— like at the university." She shook her head. "I can simply look at a person and tell if he or she is a serious student. I can see it in their faces, by the clothes they wear."

Luke just listened, keeping one eye trained on his boys.

"I think acceptance is what every person is searching for in one form or another. Love and acceptance."

"Which is what God offers us."

"Exactly—except, I didn't realize that until today." Puzzlement wafted across her freckled, feminine features. "It's so easy. Why did it seem so difficult before?"

Luke chuckled. "I know exactly where you're at. I was there, too." He pulled up a program on his laptop and handed the computer to her. "Take a look at this online Bible program. It's free and it's awesome. You can type in questions and get answers directly from God's Word. You can even search by topic."

"That's awesome."

Just then Aaron and Brian began quarreling. Devin attempted to break it up but only made things worse. Luke stood and walked to the pool to settle the matter before someone drowned.

"Daddy, it's my turn to play with the water worm." Brian pouted and pointed to the Styrofoam floatation toy.

Luke noticed his son's lips were tinged with blue and the boy shivered, not entirely out of agitation.

Dipping his hand in the water, Luke decided the pool's temperature was still rather cold. He'd filled it with the garden hose earlier, but the frigid water had felt rather good in the heat of the day. Now, however, the sun had moved to another part of the yard.

"I think you guys have had enough swimming for today."

They protested in unison.

Luke relented. "Okay, take one last dunk while I fetch some towels." He glanced at Ciara. "Would you mind keeping an eye on them?"

"Of course not."

He jogged to the house and let himself inside. He had to pause and praise the Lord for the miracle that occurred in Ciara's heart today. It went beyond his fondest hopes, his wildest imaginings.

Taking the stairs two at a time, he reached the linen closet in the hallway between two of the three bedrooms. But just as he grabbed an armful of clean towels, Ciara's shriek split the quiet summer afternoon.

Luke raced back to the first floor, but as he reached the kitchen, curiosity replaced his alarm. His kids were belly laughing. As he looked out the back door, he saw the reason why.

There in the middle of the pool sat Ciara, fully clothed and pushing the water out of her eyes.

"What in the world's going on out here?" He crossed the patio, chuckling because his sons were still cracking up over whatever it was that had happened.

Aaron could hardly speak, he laughed so hard. "Miss Ciara... sh–she splashed us."

"Yeah, big time," Devin chortled.

"Oh?" Luke arched a brow.

"Water's a little chilly, Luke."

"Yeah, I could have told you that." He swallowed another chuckle.

"But it feels sorta good." She lazed back in the pool, purposely knocking Devin off balance.

He hollered in fun and fell over, like a dramatic little clown.

The twins were in stitches.

Ciara laughed along with them. "Good babysitter that I am, I figured if you can't beat 'em, join 'em."

sixteen

The night air hung thick around Cici and Luke as they sat side by side on his cement patio, the cushion from the chaise lounge beneath them. Their backs were up against the cement stoop as they watched the flames dance in the fire pit. Luke had draped his arm around Cici's shoulder. She felt the warmth of his palm on her skin as he slowly, methodically rubbed her arm. Snuggling beside him, she thought it all seemed so perfect. In fact this whole evening had been perfect, from eating a pizza supper with Luke and his boys to watching a DVD with them and, finally, tucking the little superheroes into bed.

And now, being here, like this, with him. . .

"Luke?"

"Hmm?"

"I think I'm falling in love with you." She leaned her forehead against his jaw.

"I feel the same way, but it scares me a little."

She brought her head back. "What do you mean?"

"I dream about you, Ciara. I think about you all day long. You consume my thoughts. Sometimes I wonder if that's healthy."

"Oh, Luke. . ." She turned and placed her hand on the side of his face before bringing her lips to his. As always, a feeling that they belonged together filled her being.

Luke gathered her in his arms. The kiss deepened.

"Hello?"

A woman's voice, and its amused tone, shattered the intimacy of the moment.

"So sorry to interrupt." Another female's voice.

Cici squinted past the fire pit and into the night. "Bridget? Tanya?"

They stepped out of the shadows, giggling like teenagers.

"Ceece, we're sorry to barge in on you like this." Tanya spoke up first. "We just decided to grab some dinner at that comedy club in Des Moines, and we wondered if you'd like to come along."

"But we can tell you're sort of busy." Bridget laughed again. Her earlier dark mood had obviously blown over.

Cici glanced at Luke. "Meet my roommates."

He scrambled to his feet. "Hi."

Cici could tell he was embarrassed.

"Can I get you something to drink? A can of soda? Bottle of water?"

"Don't invite them to stay." Cici meant the remark in fun. "They just might."

"I'll take anything diet."

"Me, too."

"See?" Cici raised her hands in a helpless gesture. "What did I tell you?"

Luke headed for the kitchen, chuckling.

She turned back to her friends. "Nice going."

"We'll leave if you really want us to." Bridget sounded sincere. She brushed her blond hair back, made a ponytail, and then let it fall again, a practice she often did when she felt uncomfortable. "And I'm sorry for snapping."

"Not a problem and no, don't go. Luke and I agreed to take things slow between us and, um, I guess we were moving awfully fast there."

"I'm shocked. Talk about role reversal." Tanya dragged a lawn chair closer to where Cici still sat on the cushion. "It's usually you walking in on one of us."

"Yes, except I lived there."

Bridget, too, found a chair. "We tried to call, Ceece, but you didn't answer your cell."

"You were obviously *preoccupied*."

Cici puffed out an exasperated breath. "Oh, stop teasing me. And please don't tease Luke. He's a sweetheart of a guy."

Luke returned with two plastic cups and handed them to Bridget and Tanya. "Diet cola on the rocks."

They murmured their thanks, and he reclaimed his seat beside Cici.

"So how long have you lived next door to Jen?"

"Ever since she moved in."

Cici liked his easy tone. She felt certain her friends would find him charming and personable.

They chatted just minutes longer before a booming voice split the night. "Hey's this where the party's at?"

Chase sauntered into the yard, Jeremy in tow, and Cici wondered why the little boy wasn't in bed, sleeping.

"Mind if I join you?"

Luke, ever the polite host, stood and found another lawn chair for Chase. Meanwhile, Cici scooted over and offered the end of the cushion to Jeremy. He plunked himself down.

"Where's Devin and Aaron and Brian?"

"They're in bed for the night." *And you should be, too,* she wanted to say, although it wasn't her place.

"Bridget, Tanya, I'd like you to meet another resident of Blossomwood Estates, Chase Tibbits."

"How do, ladies."

Cici watched her roommates greet him in all politeness.

Another conversation ensued, Bridget and Tanya each taking a turn to tell both Chase and Luke a little about themselves. Cici listened on and then, to her surprise, Jeremy curled up and put his head in her lap. He was sleeping in minutes.

Cici glanced at Luke. He'd brought his legs up so that he leaned on his knees. He caught her gaze and then spied Jeremy.

She inched closer to him. "Could he sleep on your couch? Maybe he'd be more comfortable."

Luke considered the idea.

Chase must have overheard her. "Is that kid sleeping?"

Cici cringed at his gruffness.

"Listen, if it's okay with you, Jeremy can bunk with my boys tonight. I'll put a sleeping bag down on the floor."

"Well, I guess. . ."

"He's coming to Bible school with us again tomorrow morning."

"Yeah, okay. He can stay. Clothes should be clean. He had to change after dinner because he spilled milk all over himself at dinner. Clumsy kid."

"He's not clumsy, Chase. All children spill."

"Adults spill, too," Bridget pointed out.

Luke roused the boy, who nodded to the question about "camping out" with Devin, Brian, and Aaron. Then he gathered the child in his arms and stood. Cici pushed to her feet and followed Luke into the house, intending to lend a hand.

But Luke proved himself sufficient. He lent Jeremy a pair of Devin's pajamas and collected and folded up the youngster's jeans and T-shirt for tomorrow.

Jeremy yawned and crawled into the sleeping bag and put his head on the stuffed animal pillow.

Luke tousled his hair. "Everything's fine, buddy. Sleep well."

"Okay."

Cici backed up as Luke tiptoed from the room. His children didn't even stir.

"I feel sorry for that little boy. I think Chase is mean to him."

Luke reached out and caressed her cheek. "He'll be all right."

Somehow his touch made Cici believe him.

Placing a hand at the small of her back, Luke guided her to the steps. "VBS really tuckers kids out, what with all the games and activities. Parents like Chase sometimes don't realize that fact."

"Single dads like Chase aren't in tune with their children's feelings."

They walked back downstairs.

"You're generalizing again. I mean, you don't know that's the case with Chase and his kid."

She paused before they reached the kitchen. "Well, I'd like to find out. If I'm right, Chase is the perfect example to prove my thesis—at least in part. I've agreed to be objective and I haven't forgotten that."

"I'd say now's a perfect time for researching your theory, all very discreetly, of course."

Cici smiled. "Of course, although Bridget and Tanya will know what I'm up to right away."

Luke didn't reply and, as they made their way out into the backyard, Cici wondered why.

❧

Fiddling with a twig, Luke tensed as Ciara tossed another question at Chase. He didn't mind her research per se. In fact he admired the way she'd been up front about her motives. No sneaky reporting. But what bothered Luke as he listened to Ciara question Chase was that she sounded so *interested* in the guy.

It bugged him, even though Luke reminded himself that she'd just admitted to falling in love with him. Likewise, when he looked into Ciara's eyes, he thought he glimpsed forever. When he kissed her, he'd felt almost complete again for the first time since Alissa's death.

Maybe that's why he felt so vulnerable, too; Ciara held that proverbial key to his heart. Could he trust her with it?

She worked her hand around his elbow now as the last of the embers dwindled in the fire pit. Her touch bolstered his confidence; however, he couldn't seem to completely shake his insecure feelings.

"Wow, it's almost ten o'clock." Tanya stood. "If we want to make that late show at the comedy club, we'd better hustle."

"Oh, right." Bridget stood also. "Want to come with us, Chase? We're driving into Des Moines to have a few drinks and some laughs."

"Yeah, sure, I'm all about drinks and laughs with pretty

ladies." He stood and stretched. "Don't have to worry about my kid, thanks to Luke."

"Sure. Anytime." Luke pitched him a cordial grin.

"What about you, Cici?" Chase squared his shoulders. "Coming with us? You can ask me more questions about how I raise my kid."

"No, thanks."

Luke turned to her. "Don't stay behind on my account. I plan to go inside and call it a night. I'm beat." He held his breath, wondering if she'd go and praying she'd stay.

"No, I have to write my thesis. I haven't worked on it in days." She looked at her roommates. "Hear me, girls? I said *days.*"

They both feigned heart attacks and Luke chuckled. How could he possibly think he had anything to worry about where Ciara was concerned?

Even so, he felt like an actor with opening night jitters. After all, this scene was all too familiar to him. The friends. The going out. The "drinks," the "laughs"—and the tragic ending.

Chase grew impatient. "Hey, if we're going, let's get a move on."

"Yep, time to go." Ciara shooed them out of the yard like pigeons. "Thanks for stopping. Next time call first."

"Next time keep your cell phone with you," one of her roomies retorted.

Their laughter echoed between the condos.

Ciara returned, still smiling. "See what fruitcakes I live with and why I begged Jen to let me stay at her place this summer?"

Luke stood and regarded her with an appreciative gaze. He thought she was beautiful, graceful, delicate, even in faded blue jeans and a white sleeveless shirt with her curly hair springing out from its ponytail. He suspected Ciara was one of those women who could wear a potato sack and still look lovely, and if Luke knew it, other men had to see it, also. Like Chase Tibbits.

"Weren't you tempted to go out with them? You need some fun in your life, too."

"I had fun today, acting silly with your kids." She laughed and tossed her head toward the swimming pool that still stood in the middle of the yard. "And the luncheon today was enjoyable. I've had a great day."

Luke folded his arms and leaned against the side of the fence. "So you don't go out with your roommates?"

"I have on occasion." She began folding lawn chairs. "But Bridget and Tanya seem to have more energy than I do, not to mention they're both a little on the nocturnal side. Me, on the other hand, I'm up at the crack of dawn."

"Yeah, me too." Luke felt suddenly at a loss for words. He didn't want to part company, but it was getting late.

"I suppose in lieu of the fact we're both early risers we should say good night, huh?"

"I suppose."

She tipped her head. "Everything all right? You don't seem yourself."

"I think maybe I'm overtired. VBS exhausts us parents as well as the kids." It was the honest truth.

"Ah. . ." Beneath the radiant, white beam from the neighbor's yard light, he saw her smile. "Understandable." She stepped forward and slipped her arms around his waist. Luke touched her hair and traced his finger alongside her upturned face. "I can tell you're exhausted."

He felt her breath on his chin. "Yeah. . ." She pressed her lips to his in a quick kiss that left him longing for more.

"Then I shall say, as they do in Italy, *arrivederci*."

"Doesn't that mean good-bye?" Why did that pluck such a sad cord in Luke's heart?

"You're right." Ciara scrunched up her features, deep in thought. "I helped Jen learn some Italian for her trip—what's the word for good night?"

"Buona notte."

"That's it." Smiling, she took a step backward. "Buona notte, Luke."

He watched her walk around the fence. "G'night, Ciara."

seventeen

The writer's block lifted and suddenly Cici's fingers danced across her computer's keyboard.

Some single fathers consider it a burden or a nuisance to care for their children. They equate parenting to paying child support: It's a necessary evil. These inconsequential fathers become victims of their own selfishness. Cici thought about Chase Tibbits and how he seemed so eager to allow Jeremy to attend VBS and spend the night at Luke's place so he could shirk his responsibility and party. After speaking with him last night, Cici understood the man would rather let a congregation of a church and a neighbor take over caring for his son so he wasn't inconvenienced. *This anti-nurturing mentality and its subsequent actions burden society and create within the child feelings of rejection.*

She sat back and reread the paragraph. She smiled, thinking Aggie would be so proud. As for Chase, any trace of respect she might have had for him had vanished last night. And Luke? She smiled, deciding that he was an exemplary role model. Not a perfect dad, of course, but he loved his boys.

Other single fathers build their lives around their children—

The doorbell rang and Cici glanced at her wristwatch. Just after high noon. As she made her way to the front entrance, she half expected to see Luke standing just beyond the screen door.

Instead she found Chase Tibbits.

"Hey, I need your help."

"Oh?" She took in his disheveled appearance, unshaven jaw, mussed hair, swollen red eyes, and the same clothes he wore last night. "Hung over? Need aspirin or something?"

He ignored her cynicism. "Jeremy's missing."

"What?" Cici stepped out of the condo. "How can he be missing? He's with Luke's kids."

Chase shook his head. "One of Luke's kids is missing, too."

Cici's hand flew to her mouth, but she couldn't conceal her gasp of alarm.

"Luke just called to tell me. He and everyone else at church are searching for the boys right now."

"Which one of Luke's sons is it—just so I know who I'm about to go looking for?"

"I don't know. He said the kid's name—one of the younger ones."

"Aaron?"

"I think that's him."

Cici figured so, the mischievous little superhero. Her insides twisted with worry.

"I called Roberta Rawlings. She vowed to scour the entire complex just in case the kids happened to walk this far from the church."

"What time did they go missing?"

"No one's exactly sure. Bible school ended at eleven thirty. The boys were supposedly on the playground with other kids. I'm told there was adult supervision. But Luke said when he went to pick them up and bring them home, one of his boys and Jeremy were missing."

Cici lifted her gaze to the summer sky. "Please don't let anything happen to them." Her prayer was but a whisper.

Chase caught her wrist. "Come on."

She tossed reason to the wind, leaving her computer turned on, her purse and cell phone behind, and the condo unlocked. Nothing seemed to matter except finding Jeremy and Aaron unharmed.

Cici climbed up into Chase's pickup. "Where do you think Jeremy would go?"

"This isn't Jeremy's fault." He fired up the engine.

"I never said it was anyone's fault."

"I trusted Luke with my kid, and he or some other adults

should have been watching him. I'm thinking about suing."

"Think about finding your son first." Cici pulled the seat belt across her chest. "And bear with me. I'm trying to guess two little boys' thoughts. I know Aaron's got an adventurous streak. Does Jeremy?"

"Maybe. . .I mean, he is a boy. All boys are adventurous, I guess."

"That helps a lot, Chase."

He obviously caught her sarcasm and cleared his throat. "Jeremy's a good kid. He knows if he gets out of line he'll have me to deal with."

Cici fixed her gaze on Chase's meaty hands as they tightened around the steering wheel. She recalled how intimidated, even frightened, Chase had made her feel in the past, and she wondered if he ever abused Jeremy. Then she recalled the verbal mistreatment that she'd witnessed last week at the ice cream parlor.

"Do you think Jeremy would try to run away? Maybe Aaron felt compelled to help him."

"Stop blaming this on Jeremy." He pounded the wheel. "I'm worried sick about my kid. Can't you see that?"

"Truthfully? I see an angry, selfish man right now." Cici couldn't believe her own audacity. Now was not the time to pick a fight with Chase Tibbits. One wrong swerve, and he could kill them both. Even so, she had to speak the truth as she saw it.

Much to her amazement, Chase seemed humbled by the remark. "You think I'm a bad father. Well, maybe I am. Kids don't come with directions, like my power tools. Can't ask a buddy to show you how it works, and you can't take it back to the store if you don't like it after you try it out."

Cici listened, her heart breaking for Jeremy. It seemed Chase was saying he didn't love his son.

Or was he merely admitting that he didn't know *how* to love his son?

Several moments went by in silence before Chase seemed

to give himself a mental shake. "What am I thinking?" He turned the truck around.

"Where are we going?"

"I just realized that maybe we should stay at my place in case Jeremy shows up or someone tries to call me with his whereabouts."

Seemed like a good idea.

"I guess I didn't have my wits about me. All I could think of was that I had to find my kid."

"Ditto." Cici had to admit her thought pattern hadn't been the most strategic, either. But the urgency of the situation still caused the adrenaline to shoot through her veins and hasten her actions.

She decided to call Luke right away and find out where she should be searching or what else she might do to help.

They reached Chase's condo and he parked. Getting out of his pickup, she followed him inside. The place looked like an antiquated bachelor pad, as if Chase's ninety-year-old great-uncle had died and left him his furniture. Messes lay everywhere, from used paper plates and plastic cups on the coffee table to clothes strewn about the living room and a laundry basket at the foot of the stairs.

"Can I use your phone?"

"On the desk, over there."

Cici strode across the beige carpeting and moved a pile of unopened mail to get to the cordless device. Lifting the receiver, she thought it smelled like rancid beer.

"Hey, what do you know; Luke's here."

She dropped the phone and rushed to the doorway. She looked around Chase to see Luke open the sliding van door. Four boys jumped out—including Aaron and Jeremy.

Elation bubbled up inside her, and she pushed past Chase to get outside. She jogged across the lawn and gathered Jeremy in one arm and Aaron in the other. "Thank God you guys are all right!" After hugging them close, she pulled back. "Where have you been?" She looked at Aaron.

His brown eyes stared back at her in all innocence. "He wanted his mom. I had to help him find her."

Cici pressed her lips together and gazed at Jeremy.

"I want to go home." He pouted. "I don't want to stay with my dad anymore. I want my mom."

"Well, you still shouldn't have run off like that—either one of you."

Hearing Luke's voice, she flicked her gaze at him. He stood by, hands on his hips, watching the scene unfold. His usually soft, soulful eyes looked like polished mahogany. But what had she expected? Luke had just been through quite a scare. No doubt he was upset and stifling his emotions until later when he could express them.

Chase stepped up beside her and began to berate his son. "What's up with taking off like that? Don't you have a brain in your head?"

"Must you be such a brute?" She instinctively hugged Jeremy to her. "Instead of yelling at him, why don't you tell your son how much the thought of losing him forever scared you?" Taking the boy by the shoulders, she made him face his dad. "Tell him how proud you are of him, Chase, because he can hang by his knees and do all sorts of really cool things. Tell him he's special. Tell him you want him to be part of your life. . .tell him that you—you love him."

Chase swallowed hard before he hunkered down. He stared at his boy. Seconds later, he enveloped his son in a bear-like hug. The sight caused tears to well in Cici's eyes.

She turned her attention to Aaron and put an arm around his shoulder. "You scared me to pieces."

He leaned against her hip, as if in silent apology.

"Scared us, too," Devin said.

Brian bobbed his head in agreement.

The kids closed in for a group hug, and it was then that Cici wished Luke's sons were hers, also. She wished Luke was her husband, and they were one big, happy family.

Could that really happen to her? Love? A family?

"I know you scared your dad to pieces, too." Again, she glanced at Luke. Stepping toward him, she touched his arm. "You okay?"

"I'll be fine."

She thought he averted his gaze. But why?

"I'd better get these boys home." He lifted Aaron out of her arms and set him inside the van. Devin and Brian scrambled in after him.

"Can I help you feed the kids lunch? In fact, I'll watch the boys this afternoon and give you a break."

"I can manage." Luke closed the sliding door. "Besides, Chase needs you more than I do."

"What?" Cici didn't think she heard him correctly. She turned to see Chase carry his son into the condo before looking back at Luke. "What's that supposed to mean?"

Without a word, he climbed behind the wheel, closed the door, and drove up the block. Cici could do nothing but watch him go.

☙

Luke heard the faint knock at the back door but ignored it. He knew Ciara wanted to talk, but he just didn't feel like discussing anything with her at the moment. He'd experienced a wide gamut of emotions today and he didn't think he could handle much more. He'd been terrified when Aaron and Jeremy were reported missing. Then with a sickening dread, he'd phoned Chase with the news. Minutes later, once Devin and Brian were situated in the van, he'd tried to reach Ciara but was disappointed she didn't answer her cell. When he spied the two boys in a nearby subdivision, Luke had never known such elation. Jeremy had gotten homesick and thought he knew the way to his mother's house, but he was afraid to walk there alone, so Aaron volunteered to escort him—taking his superhero role too seriously.

Luke spent the afternoon talking to his sons about the dangers of wandering off. He explained, grilled and drilled them, and all three crossed their hearts and promised to always tell him or another trusted adult where they were going.

He rejoiced that the outcome was a good one. Still, he was haunted by the interest Ciara had shown in Chase last night. Then the sight of her today, with Chase, leaving the condo with him. . .

Luke felt physically ill each time the memory played back. Why had he ever entertained the notion that he'd be enough for her, that she'd be satisfied with his less-than-exciting way of life?

And then the effect she had on his bawdy neighbor. Amazing, really. She'd reached him in a significant way today. When Chase finally embraced his son, her eyes filled with joy.

Except Luke hadn't put it there—Chase did.

An overwhelming swell of gloom lodged in his chest. But he figured it was better to come to grips with the truth now and sever his relationship with Ciara than to relive the nightmare that had resulted from Alissa's wanderlust.

Another light *tap, tap-tap* sounded at the door, but just as before, he refused to answer it.

eighteen

What a big baby!

Cici wasn't sure if she was more irritated or hurt that Luke had been dodging her for a week. But she finally gave up trying to corner him to explain herself. She'd deduced that Luke had jumped to inaccurate conclusions about her and Chase and now his insecurity had overtaken his common sense. But if he wouldn't listen, how could she set him straight?

A few more days passed, and Cici tried to consume herself with her thesis; however, on a Friday afternoon, after a frustrating appointment with her professor, she arrived back at Jen's condo to find Luke in his driveway. He'd loaded suitcases, sleeping bags, and pillows into his van.

He froze when he saw her coming up the walk.

"Looks like you're going somewhere."

"I decided to spend a month in Minnesota, visiting my folks." He turned and resumed packing. "Need to get away."

"From me? But I've been trying to let you have your space." When he didn't reply, an indescribable sorrow sank into her heart. Her hopes to discuss the situation with Luke before Jen returned home vanished. "Oh, fine, Luke. Have it your way. I thought you'd be a decent enough guy to flat-out tell me your feelings had changed—or at the very least, *say good-bye*."

She fought the familiar angst of abandonment. Her father hadn't bothered to say good-bye, either. One day he just up and left.

"Luke?"

He closed the hatch with a forceful shove. "I've got to get the kids in the van and hit the road. We've got a long drive ahead of us."

Disappointment and confusion assailed her. But what more could she say—that she'd been right about him and every other man on the planet?

She swung around and saw Tori Evenrod and Michayla Martinelli across the street. They looked her way and waved, and Cici suspected her voice had carried a little too far, and now her relationship with Luke and its heart-crunching demise would soon be the talk of Blossomwood Estates.

Great. Just great. She returned the wave and pushed out a friendly smile as if nothing were wrong. Nothing at all.

ॐ

The month of August progressed miserably for Luke— and it had nothing to do with the humid weather and the mosquitoes or the fact that he came down with a bout of the flu and lost an important client. He felt like both Job and Jonah combined, what with his trials and running from God. He was only too grateful that his parents picked up the slack.

"Why don't you just move back home here where you belong?" His mother, plump with short dark hair, moved about the kitchen as she prepared dinner. She peeked out the window to where the boys played in the yard. "The boys love it here, they can run free, and I could take care of all of you. I'd feed you, make sure you had clean clothes. You'd have more time to concentrate on your work. I mean, what's in Iowa anyway?"

"Not a baseball or football team, that's for sure," Dad groused from behind a section of the newspaper.

"Alissa's family's there. They help me out when they can. My church is there. My friends. . ."

Ciara.

"They can all come visit. Lord knows there's plenty of room in this old farmhouse. And if they don't want to stay in the house, we'll set up the camper."

Somehow Luke couldn't envision his rather persnickety in-laws in either a farmhouse with no central air conditioning or a pop-top camper.

His father must have guessed his thoughts. "There's always the hotel in town for those who don't want to *rough it*."

Luke had to chuckle.

Dad rustled the pages of the newspaper before setting it in a heap on the table. "So what's really eating you?"

"Besides the bugs?"

"Yeah. Besides the bugs." His father regarded him over his bifocals. His keen, walnut brown eyes pierced Luke in a way that made him want to confess.

"Okay, okay. . .there's this woman—"

"I knew it!" Mom hurried across the room and sat down beside Luke. "I knew it was a woman. Didn't I say that, Daniel?"

"Yeah, you might have mentioned something along those lines." Dad ran a hand over his graying short hair.

"So who is she, what's she like. . .and why are you acting so lovesick?"

"Mom." Luke bristled. Despite his best efforts and accomplishments in life, his mother still treated him like he was in high school. Little wonder he didn't want to move back to Minnesota. "In all due respect, will you just cool it?"

She sat back in her chair and pressed her lips together.

Luke rubbed his jaw. On one hand he was thankful his mother loved him. Some guys only wished their mothers cared about them. Still, Luke had to draw the line with her from time to time. He was just glad she had grandchildren to absorb that overexuberant motherliness left over from raising him and his brothers.

With a sigh of resignation, Luke began telling his folks about Ciara, how they met, how she came to know Christ and believe, and how they fell in love.

And, yes, he did love her.

"The kids adored her. Aaron even started talking about having a mom. . ."

"Oh, Luke." His mother's fingers fluttered to the base of her neck.

"But everything seems so impossible between Ciara and me now. I want to think it's for the best, but somehow I can't accept it."

Mom set a hand on his forearm. "Why not give her a call?"

Luke gave her an incredulous look. "She'll hang up on me. I mean, I'd hang up on me if I was her."

"Then send her an e-mail," Dad suggested. "You're a computer guy. Send her one of those fancy Internet cards."

"Or a text message on her cell phone."

"And say what? I'm insecure because of what happened with Alissa so I acted out by behaving like an insensitive jerk?"

"That'd be a start." Mom smiled, leaned over, and kissed his cheek. "That'd be a very good start."

❧

"The pictures and DVD from your trip are amazing." Cici sat forward and took a sip of her hot, spicy tea. It was hard to believe the summer had flown by and Jen and William were back in Iowa. The Labor Day weekend was just days away.

"I'll never forget it." Sitting cross-legged on the carpet, Jen flicked strands of her silky, golden-brown hair off one slender shoulder. "And sharing all those new experiences with the man I love"—she sent William an adoring look—"made everything all the more special."

Cici glanced over in time to see him reply to Jen with an affectionate wink. She shifted on the sofa, feeling like the fifth wheel on a wagon. "I suppose I should get going." She stood. "I have a meeting with Aggie tomorrow, except I don't know why. She already disapproved of my thesis and said she won't recommend me to my committee of professors."

"I read the draft of your thesis that you e-mailed me earlier in the week." William pushed to his feet. "I'm still impressed. You laid out examples of bad and good parenting, cited why single fathers are disadvantaged from a societal viewpoint, and then ended on a hopeful note. You allowed readers to form their own assumptions. Excellent."

"I wish you were my professor." Still, Cici felt satisfied with her achievement, and the fact that William complimented her work took some of the sting out of Aggie's discouraging assessment. In a word, Aggie *hated* it. The trouble had all begun when Cici changed the title of her thesis back in early July, and things with Aggie went downhill from there.

"Well, at least you stayed true to what you believe." Jen sprang up from where she'd been sitting on the floor. "I'm proud of you."

"Thanks, except it's doubtful I'll earn my master's now."

"What a shame." Stepping forward, she slung one long, slim arm around Cici's shoulders. "I know you worked so hard. But you took the high road and didn't compromise on what you know is true. That takes courage."

Cici shrugged her reply. "I don't know how brave I am, but at least I was offered a job with the county's department of education. It's not the one I had my eye on, but it'll pay the bills."

"Congratulations!" Jen gave her a little hug.

"See, God came through for you in spite of that professor." William smiled.

"The job is answered prayer, that's for sure."

Jen released a happy sigh. "And to think you're not just my best friend in the whole world now, you're my sister, adopted into the family of Christ. I don't think I've ever been so happy as when I learned you became a Christian, aside from the day William proposed to me, of course."

"Of course." Seeing the joy on Jen's face made Cici smile, too, although she continued to grapple with various biblical truths. Like, what if God decided He didn't want her in His family? Would He dump her like her dad and Luke had? No reply. No explanation. Just here one day and gone the next?

"Cici, as long as we're on the subject of your conversion. . ." William stepped forward. "Part of being a Christian is learning and growing by hearing God's Word. So, I'd like to invite you to come to church with us on Sunday."

"No way." Cici shook her head for emphasis.

"Oh, Cici." Jen looked disappointed. "We're a friendly

congregation. You can sit with William and me."

"I've been to your church. I like your pastor and all the people. I especially enjoyed meeting Jesse and Mandy Satlock this summer. It's just that. . .I don't want to run into Luke." She shrugged off Jen's arm and lifted her mug of tea from the coffee table. "The only reason I came over here tonight is because he's still gone."

"So you only became a Christian because of Luke?" William stood with his arms akimbo.

"No, I didn't. And for your information, I plan to attend Sunday service at a small church near the university. Tanya expressed interest in attending with me. For myself, I knew it was the right place because it was like God spoke to only me when I glimpsed a wood engraving on the altar. It read: *I will never leave you nor forsake you.*"

"And He never will, either." Earnestness narrowed Jen's gaze.

Cici smiled. "Well, I'm willing to give Him a chance. As for Luke. . .what can I say?"

"The two of you need to talk." William seemed determined.

"I've tried talking to Luke numerous times. He either gives me curt answers or doesn't reply at all. Then he left without even saying good-bye. He knows I've struggled with abandonment issues in the past. He wanted to hurt me on purpose." She headed for the kitchen, intending to dump her unfinished tea in the sink. Her heart ached just thinking about Luke. Despite his hateful actions, she missed him and his precious children.

"I know Luke. He wouldn't hurt you on purpose." William's deep voice wafted in from the living room. "Sounds to me like he was being selfish and only thought about himself and his own feelings."

Both he and Jen came to stand in the kitchen archway.

"Luke got jealous and for no good reason." Cici turned from the sink. "Although, I understand in part. There is history behind Luke's feelings of insecurity because of how his wife died. I'm willing to work through it with him. But he's shut me out of his life and that. . ." She swallowed hard. "Hurts so much."

Her friends grew thoughtful for several long moments.

"I wonder what Luke will say when he finds out Chase and Bridget are dating." Jen had to smile.

A grin pulled at William's mouth. "Maybe that'll quell Luke's jealousy once and for all."

"I doubt it." Cici folded her arms. "I think Luke needs something more along the lines of counseling."

"He knows the Almighty Counselor."

"Maybe Luke's shunning Him, too." Cici rolled her eyes.

Jen shook her head, looking amazed. "Chase and Bridget? Who would have thought it? They suit each other, you know? Rough around the edges, but big softies inside."

"If you want to know the truth, they're both getting on my nerves *big time*." Cici couldn't help venting. "They're together all the time." She flung up her hands in frustration. "Oh, maybe I'm the one who's jealous now. I wish Luke and I were a couple."

"At least you can admit it," William said.

Cici shrugged.

Jen stepped closer to her, compassion etched into her every feature. "I'm sorry you're hurting. You're my friend and I love you."

Cici's eyes filled.

"As for Chase and Bridget, if they bother you, you can move in with me for a while."

"What? You and William are more the lovebirds than Chase and Bridget." Cici laughed in spite of herself. "Seriously, thanks, Jen, I appreciate the offer, but no—especially with Luke living next door."

"But you know you're going to have to face him, hopefully sooner rather than later."

Cici tipped her head, curious.

Jen's eyes widened. "I'm getting married in a month."

"I know. I'm happy and excited for you."

"You don't understand." Jen blinked. "Both you and Luke are standing up in the wedding!"

nineteen

Luke dropped the boys off at school. Devin started first grade this year and the twins began half-day kindergarten. They weren't babies anymore. Pretty soon they'd be driving.

He winced. The thought gave his heart a jump start. It also served as a reminder that he didn't want to journey through life alone, but he almost believed he was incapable of trusting another woman with his love.

Pulling into the driveway, Luke parked the van and got out. As he made his way toward the front door, he spotted Jen who, judging by her professional attire, was leaving for work. They'd only briefly chatted since he arrived home yesterday—Labor Day.

He waved.

She waved back. "Say a prayer for Cici. She starts her new job today."

Luke almost missed a step at the mention of Ciara's nickname, but he grinned politely nonetheless.

Jen didn't say anything more as she climbed into her sand-colored coupe. Her tone had been so nonchalant that Luke wondered how much, if anything, she knew about the situation between him and Ciara.

Say a little prayer. . .

Luke had been speaking with the Lord, but he hadn't felt a particular leading, although his senses seemed to petrify each time he considered contacting Ciara.

She starts a new job today.

He unlocked the front door and let himself inside. More than a month had gone by since he'd last seen or spoken to her. Had she finished her thesis?

I've got no right to ask.

Luke walked upstairs to his home office. He shook off his thoughts of Ciara and did his best to focus on a new program he'd recently sold to a local company. Around lunchtime he heard the mail arrive and went to get it. The house seemed far too quiet, what with Devin in school all day and the twins at the Satlocks' for the afternoon. He was grateful that Mandy offered to help him out three days a week. Even so, the silence would take some getting used to.

He ambled out to the mailbox at the curb and sifted through the envelopes as he made his way back to the house. Glimpsing Ciara's name and her apartment's address, he halted in mid stride. A second later, he tore into the large, square envelope, too curious to even wait until he was inside.

Dear Luke. . .Seeing as we're both in Jen and William's wedding party, I'd like to formally ask you to agree to look beyond ourselves and focus on celebrating our friends' special day. I ask this so neither one of us will feel awkward and uncomfortable. . .

Luke blew out a breath and continued his trek inside. He'd forgotten all about it, not the wedding or agreeing to be one of William's groomsmen, but the fact that he and Ciara would be together in some capacity for the occasion.

Collapsing into the sofa, he regarded the colorful blank card in which she'd scribed her proposed "agreement." He felt both foolish and wrung out emotionally, but the least she deserved was an apology and a promise that he'd be cordial and friendly at the wedding next month.

As for himself, he recognized now as the time to call his pastor and seek out godly counsel. Life was just too short to live in misery.

❧

Cici parked her car and walked through the lot to her apartment. Only the first week of September and already it felt like fall. Low humidity, temperatures in the upper seventies. It almost seemed like summer had never existed. July she associated with falling in love with Luke and August with nursing her heartbreak. Both months were best forgotten—so that took care of the majority of her summer.

But at least she enjoyed her new job.

Taking the stairs to her second-story unit, Cici decided she couldn't wait to kick off her shoes. After being barefoot or in flip-flops for the last few months, leather pumps with a three-inch heel for nine hours a day took some adjustment.

"Look what came for you today!"

Cici had barely gotten into the apartment when Bridget made the announcement. Surrounded by textbooks on the couch, her blond roommate nodded toward the coffee table and the beautiful bouquet of pink and purple orchids with curly willows added for decoration.

Cici set down her purse and work bag. "For me?"

"Yep. But I couldn't even snoop to find out who sent them because the card attached is in a sealed envelope. But I'll bet the flowers are from Luke. Either him or your cranky professor. Maybe she's sorry she trashed your thesis."

"Are you kidding? Aggie doesn't apologize to *anyone*. But, you know what? I'm okay with it." Cici tore into the envelope. "I'm all about pleasing God, not her."

"Way to go."

Cici read the type-printed card. *The words "I'm sorry" didn't seem like enough. Can you ever forgive me?*

"And? Who's the arrangement from?"

"Luke." Cici was tempted to take his flowers and toss them out the window. He'd wounded her deeply, but he was sorry—and she believed he meant the apology. What's more, he had contacted her in a positive way. She no longer had to dread seeing him at Jen and William's wedding.

Now it was time to do her part, please God, as she'd just touted, and forgive Luke.

☙

Cici's footsteps echoed in the nearly empty church parking lot. For the past month she'd felt confident about the rehearsal dinner tonight and about facing Luke. Now, however, with the moment at hand, she felt anxious flutters filling her midsection.

She entered the building and made her way to the sanctuary, but as the sole of her brown patent-leather dress shoe touched the carpeting, she heard the soft, sure timbre of Luke's voice, followed by his carefree chuckle.

She spun around on her heel—

And almost collided with Jen.

"Cici! I'm glad you're here. We're about to start. I'm trying to round up everyone."

She smiled, noticing her best friend's harried expression. "Can I help?"

"Nope. Just have a seat up front." She paused. "Oh, and I love the outfit. Can I borrow it sometime?"

"Only if you dry-clean it before giving it back." Cici grinned and some of her tension ebbed. The joke was that the russet silk dress belonged to Jen.

Continuing up the aisle, Cici slipped into the second pew from the front in the large, oval-shaped auditorium. She spotted Luke out the corner of her eye. In honor of tonight's semiformal affair, he wore a dark suit and a lavender dress shirt. He clowned around beside William, pretending to hang himself with his necktie.

She swallowed a laugh and lowered her gaze. One of the things she loved about Luke was his sense of humor. . .

"Can I have everyone's attention?"

Cici set her small handbag aside and trained her eyes on the pastor, but despite her best efforts to keep focused, she saw Luke in her peripheral vision as he sat one pew up, to her far right.

The pastor, stout with a graying goatee, continued with his instructions. They were going to practice walking down the aisle. Grandparents, parents, and then Jen's sister, the maid of honor, would step out first on the arm of the best man, William's brother. Mandy and Jesse were slated to go next, followed by Grace and Trevor Morris.

Finally it would be Cici and Luke's turn. It came as no surprise to her, after Jen listed the attendants; however, she never fathomed her legs would be so unsteady as she made her way to the back of the church.

After hellos to Mandy and Grace, she lined up beside Luke in the spacious foyer.

"Hi."

"Hi." She tried to act natural, calm, cool. He certainly seemed his jovial self as he bantered with his buddies. It seemed to take forever for the couples to make their way to the altar, but at long last they neared the entryway.

"Would you like a breath mint?"

Cici gasped. "Do I need one?" She stared at the tiny plastic container in his hand.

"No." He paled in what seemed like a mix of chagrin and horror. "I only meant to be polite, break the ice—I mean, not that there's ice, really. . ."

Cici raised her brows. A heartbeat later, she guessed his nervousness matched her own.

"I, um. . .well, what I meant is ice as in icebreaker. . ."

While he sputtered on, she helped herself to a mint, just in case. "Thanks." She popped it into her mouth.

"Sure." Luke pocketed the peppermints before offering his arm.

She threaded her hand around his elbow. Then it was step, pause, step, pause, step. . .

"Now, remember, ladies, you'll be carrying bouquets in one hand." The pastor's wife spoke the reminder into the microphone in order to be heard above all the milling around.

"Thank you for the flowers, by the way." Cici threw out an icebreaker of her own. "I enjoyed them."

Step. Pause.

"You're welcome. I wasn't sure what it meant when I didn't hear back from you."

Step. Pause.

"But," he added, "William said you were willing to forgive and forget."

Step, pause.

"He's right and I did."

In reply, Luke pressed her hand between his arm and rib cage. A subtle gesture—a token of friendship?

Step. Pause. Step.

They reached the platform and parted, Cici to the left. Luke to the right. She turned in time to watch Jen and William head for the altar. Cici's best friend glowed with happiness.

All went well for the next several minutes until Cici made the mistake of glancing across the platform at Luke. Her gaze melded to his warm brown eyes as he returned her stare. In that instant, Cici knew her feelings for Luke hadn't changed a mite.

"Cici? Would you mind handling that for the bride? Cici!"

"What?" She snapped back to reality, noticing the pastor and his wife, Jen and William, and the entire wedding party were waiting for an answer. Embarrassment crashed over her. She wasn't even sure who'd spoken. "Um. . .could someone repeat that question?"

૨ช

Rows of white linen-covered tables filled the paneled banquet room. Sitting at one of the four center tables, Luke finished the last of his apple pie, a marvelous dessert after a delicious meal of grilled rib-eye steak, homemade hash brown potatoes, and an autumn medley of stir-fried squash. Luke set aside his plate, feeling like he might burst.

Sitting back, he let his gaze wander around the dimly lit room. Strains of classical music played in the background while everywhere people mingled, some at tables and others standing in clusters. Luke searched for Ciara but didn't see her anywhere. Last he'd glimpsed her, she was sitting somewhere behind him, near the front of the room.

He slid his chair back and stood.

"Where are you going?" Mandy looked up from across the table.

Beside her, Jesse's gaze lit on him, as he sipped from his coffee cup.

"I think I'll mosey on into the lobby and walk off some of my dinner."

"Well, you might want to mosey out to the patio." Mandy threw a thumb in the direction of the bank of sliding glass doors leading outside. "I saw a certain redhead in a flattering sienna-colored dress head that way a few minutes ago."

"Thanks for the tip." Luke grinned. And thanks to Ciara's blunder at the rehearsal, he, along with everyone present, knew she had feelings for him. Her distraction had become the rolling joke all evening, but to her credit, she took it in stride, with her slim shoulders squared and her delicate chin held high. Luke had pitied her, having been the object of his friends' good-natured wisecracks in the past, but Ciara's brief preoccupation with him as they'd stood near the altar this afternoon was all the encouragement Luke needed to seek her out now. There was so much he longed to say to her.

With deliberate strides, he made his way across the banquet room and through the floor-to-ceiling glass doors. Outside, he found himself on a wood-plank, wraparound porch that overlooked the now dark golf course—deserted except for Ciara. Luke spied her slim, shadowy figure meandering along a cement walkway, her arms folded.

He seized the moment, making quick business about descending the steps around the corner and reaching her on the walk.

She heard him coming up behind her, stopped, and turned.

"Want some company?"

"Okay, sure."

Luke tried to cover his breathlessness from the sprint.

"How have you been? How's life?"

She laughed. "I'm fine and I like my new job. It's not the one I wanted, but it'll do."

"I read your thesis."

"You did?" She turned and regarded him beneath the moonlit sky.

"I inquired about it, and William forwarded the copy you sent him."

"What did you think?"

"Thought it was a commendable piece. Any single mother who reads it will feel empowered, but not at the expense of single dads. I was especially impressed by the way you handled 'Example B'—the guy who resembled Chase Tibbits. You described his parenting skills as 'loathsome' and yet you ended on a high note, explaining that even the most insensitive of men can learn to nurture their children. Great job."

"Thank you."

They walked on at a slow, unhurried pace, and seconds of silence ticked by.

"So, how are you?"

Luke didn't think he could describe what all he'd been through in a mere reply, so he settled for, "I'm okay."

"How are the boys?"

"Great." Luke told her about their experiences at school and Devin joining a soccer team.

"I miss them," she said wistfully.

"They miss you, too. Aaron talks about you all the time. For some reason he still thinks you live next door. I've explained time and time again that you were only staying there until Miss Jen got back from her trip, but. . ." Luke rolled his shoulders with uncertainty. "Maybe it's a form of denial—like the kind his old man's been plagued with for the last three-plus years."

"What?"

Luke halted and Ciara did the same.

"I've been seeing a Christian counselor. He's a friend of one of my pastors. Godly man as well as a down-to-earth guy. Counsels me from God's Word and not from his own opinions and experiences. He reminds me of my grandfather, wise and to the point." Luke paused in momentary thought. "I didn't realize how much baggage I'd been carrying around since Alissa died. But the counselor helped me see that I never had time to grieve or come to grips with the issues surrounding her death because I had three young children who needed me. Then I met you and those emotions that were stuffed away, ignored, and denied resurfaced. But I'm dealing with them."

"Oh, Luke." Ciara turned her head, glancing across the darkness that veiled the golf course before looking back at him. "I was never interested in Chase. Not ever."

"I know."

"That day Jeremy and Aaron went missing—"

Luke pressed his fingertips to her lips. "I know." He cupped her face in his hands and gently pulled her to him. "And I'm so sorry I hurt you. There are no words to express my regret." A single tear fell onto his thumb. "Don't cry."

He enveloped her in his arms and kissed her. He'd only dreamed of this moment a million times, prayed it'd come true.

"I love you, Ciara." He placed a kiss on her temple. "If you'll give me another chance, I promise I'll never hurt you or leave you—you'd be stuck with me for better or worse."

She sniffed. "I love you, too, Luke." Her voice sounded soft but thick with emotion. "I'd like nothing better than to be stuck with you." She lifted her lips to his.

He kissed her again.

twenty

You're a gorgeous bride with a perfect wedding day."

Cici swung her gaze from the full-length mirror and to her best friend. Only seven short months ago, Jen had been the one wearing white satin and lace.

Now it was Cici's turn. Today she would become Mrs. Luke Weldon. And to Cici's delight, her mother was ecstatic about becoming a grandmother.

"I'm so happy."

"With good cause." Jen, the matron of honor, adjusted Cici's veil. "I had doubts about an outdoor wedding, but the weather's perfect. It feels like summer, but it's only the end of May."

"A gift from God—you don't know how hard I prayed that He'd keep the rain away."

"Your prayers were answered, but now. . .it's time to go. William sent word saying *your sons* are racing around the yard in their tuxedoes, getting hot, sweaty, and giving their grandparents a run for their money—including your mom."

Cici wagged her head. "That's my superheroes for you."

"You sure you know what you're getting into?"

"Positive." Cici had never felt more certain of anything in her life. Being Luke's wife and his sons' mother was everything she'd ever wanted and more.

"Oh, and I should warn you: Aggie came."

"You're kidding, right?" Cici brought her chin back in surprise. She'd sent her professor an invitation but received no reply.

"Apparently, she brought a date."

"A *date?*"

"Yes, and he's a very distinguished-looking gentleman."

"Shut *up*," Cici said facetiously and Jen laughed.

"She seems quite smitten with the man. Perhaps her hard-line feminist views are softening. Maybe she'll even reconsider your thesis."

"Perhaps," Cici agreed. "But for now, God, Luke, and the boys are enough to fill up my whole life."

Jen smiled. "So, are you ready?"

"Ready."

She and Jen hugged each other, and Cici felt so blessed to have such a good friend.

Together they left the tiny fieldstone cottage, which served as the women's dressing room. Outside, sunshine spilled through budding treetops. Cici caught Devin by the collar as he made a dash past her.

"Settle down now," she whispered, brushing blades of grass off the shoulder of his black tux. "The wedding's about to start."

"Finally."

Cici smiled at his impatience and, after a kiss on the cheek, she sent him to the front of the queue.

One of Luke's cousins manned a keyboard and started playing the wedding march. The procession began, men in black tuxes and women in flowing, sea green tea-length gowns.

At last Cici walked the grassy aisle, her gaze fixed on no one but Luke. Then, standing beneath a canopy of silk gardenias, she held his hands while he recited his vows. She'd never felt more loved and cherished, and she knew each word came from his heart.

". . .to have and to hold, from this day forward, as long as we both shall live."

Luke gazed deeply into her eyes and gave her fingers a meaningful squeeze.

Then it was Cici's turn. As the pastor led her, she promised to "love, honor, and cherish."

When the vows were finished, Jen read from 1 Corinthians 13: "'Love is patient, love is kind. It does not envy, it does not boast, it is not proud. It is not rude, it is not self-seeking, it is not easily angered, it keeps no record of wrongs. Love does not delight in evil but rejoices with the truth. It always protects, always trusts, always hopes, always perseveres. Love never fails.'"

Cici knew it was true.

"I now pronounce you man and wife. Luke," the pastor said, "you may kiss your bride."

Cici smiled—until she glimpsed the mischievous spark in Luke's brown eyes.

"Be nice." She warned him without moving her lips.

"Always."

Luke drew her into his arms and then dipped her backward before pressing his lips to hers.

Their guests applauded.

"Show-off."

Luke chuckled and their sons jumped up and down, laughing.

"Do that again, Daddy." Aaron clapped his hands.

"I'll do that lots of times today."

Cici considered herself fairly warned.

Arm in arm, they walked past friends and family members who tossed birdseed at them in celebration of their union. They made their way toward the white canvas tent. Beneath its billows, the bridal party formed a line so they could greet everyone who entered the makeshift reception area for food, wedding cake, and punch.

"I love you, Ciara," Luke whispered close to her ear.

She smiled. He told her that at least twenty-five times a day. "I love you, too, but those words can't come close to expressing how I feel right now." She pressed herself close to him. "I guess I'll just have to spend the rest of our lives showing you how much I love you."

"I'll look forward to it." He kissed her again.

"All right, that's quite enough." Aggie appeared, wearing an ivory blouse and peach-colored slacks.

"I'm glad you came." Cici's eyes filled as she hugged her once-beloved professor.

Aggie only halfheartedly returned the gesture, but she'd never been one to display outward affection.

"I wish you every happiness in the world." She gave Luke an appraising glance. "You, too."

"Thank you." He inclined his head in a single, gracious move.

Aggie introduced her gentleman friend and they moved on.

Next Tori Evenrod congratulated them, followed by the lovely Michayla Martinelli.

Michayla kissed both of Cici's cheeks in a European-like fashion. "Lovely wedding, and Roberta has outdone herself once more with the amazing spread of food."

Cici agreed and, not for the first time, felt grateful for Roberta Rawlings' organizational skills.

Bridget, Chase, and Tanya stepped in front of them, congratulating both her and Luke.

"Say, who's the guy on the piano keyboard?" Tanya aimed her gaze at the man across the decorated yard.

"That's my cousin."

"Married?"

A grin crept across Luke's face. "Actually, no he's not."

"Is he a believer?"

Luke inclined his head. "He is."

"Cool." She turned and headed for the nice-looking pianist before Cici even got a hug.

Cici laughed and had to admit her former roommates would probably get their "M-r-s" degrees before Cici earned her master's. But that was fine, because she'd found joy to last a lifetime with Luke—

And three little superheroes who had once lived next door.

A Letter To Our Readers

Dear Reader:

In order that we might better contribute to your reading enjoyment, we would appreciate your taking a few minutes to respond to the following questions. We welcome your comments and read each form and letter we receive. When completed, please return to the following:

Fiction Editor
Heartsong Presents
PO Box 719
Uhrichsville, Ohio 44683

1. Did you enjoy reading *The Superheroes Next Door* by Andrea Boeshaar?
   ❑ Very much! I would like to see more books by this author!
   ❑ Moderately. I would have enjoyed it more if

   _____

   _____

   _____

2. Are you a member of **Heartsong Presents**? ❑ Yes ❑ No
   If no, where did you purchase this book? _____

   _____

3. How would you rate, on a scale from 1 (poor) to 5 (superior), the cover design? _____

4. On a scale from 1 (poor) to 10 (superior), please rate the following elements.

   _____ Heroine   _____ Plot
   _____ Hero   _____ Inspirational theme
   _____ Setting   _____ Secondary characters

5. These characters were special because? _____

_____

_____

6. How has this book inspired your life? _____

_____

_____

7. What settings would you like to see covered in future
   Heartsong Presents books? _____

_____

_____

8. What are some inspirational themes you would like to see
   treated in future books? _____

_____

_____

9. Would you be interested in reading other **Heartsong
   Presents** titles? ❑ Yes ❑ No

10. Please check your age range:

    ❑ Under 18   ❑ 18-24

    ❑ 25-34   ❑ 35-45

    ❑ 46-55   ❑ Over 55

Name_____

Occupation _____

Address _____

City, State, Zip_____

If you enjoyed

The Superhereos Next Door

then read:

DIXIE
Hearts

Southern Sympathies by Andrea Boeshaar
A Matter of Security by Kay Cornelius
The Bride Wore Coveralls by Debra Ullrick
